The Third Apprentice

Tales from Nōl'Deron

Lana Axe

AxeLord Publications
ISBN-10: 069231492X
ISBN-13: 978-0692314920

Cover art by Michael Gauss

For Eric, whose help has been invaluable.

Chapter 1

Master Imrit's cottage stood at the edge of The Barrens, far from the bustling cities of Ky'sall. He demanded vast quantities of breathing room to train his apprentices, who would achieve the rank of master under his expert tutelage. At his advanced age, dozens of such apprentices had been trained within the walls of his small cottage, and each of them had gone on to successful careers. He was highly selective about the young mages he was willing to take on, and this year had been no exception. Two mages had been selected and had proved themselves worthy students. Alongside Taren, the young mage Imrit had raised himself, they were ready to embark on their final task as apprentices. If they returned, they would return as masters of their craft.

"We must make ready! We must make ready!" the old man repeated to himself as he buzzed through his house.

Trailing behind him as always was his young, blond-haired servant Vita. She saw to the master's every need, and today was no exception. She smiled to herself to see him move so gracefully through the rooms, making sure he hadn't forgotten to give his apprentices anything they would need for their journey. Shaking her head, she attempted to suppress a grin as he dawdled here and there. Everything the apprentices needed had been prepared days ago—she had seen to that herself. Still she followed as he continued his meticulous double and triple checking of the house.

Though Vita was not a student of magic, she had grown quite fond of Master Imrit. He was a kind man and could be rather amusing at times. His treatment of her had always been kind, despite her lack of status. A servant wasn't usually treated so well in Ky'sall. Vita considered herself lucky to have Imrit as her employer. Despite being so far from the cities where she had grown up, she enjoyed her life and work here at the edge of the woods.

"There it is, there it is," he mumbled. "I almost forgot." Picking up a small phial from the cupboard, he stuffed it down into his pocket. "That's for later," he said, winking at the girl. "Now, where are my apprentices? This is their big day, after all."

"They're crafting the last of their potions," she informed him. "Or they were, last I checked." She had been following Imrit through the house for nearly an hour, so she hadn't laid eyes on the apprentices in at least that long. Chances were, they were still upstairs.

"Well, hurry and bring them down!" Imrit scolded. "I can't wait all day!" Though his tone was gruff, his face held back a smile. All his life he had dreamed of this day, and now it had arrived. The finest apprentices he had ever trained were setting out, and they would return with the object he desired most—one that could grant him eternal life.

Vita hurried up the stairs and quietly knocked on the door to the laboratory. It creaked slightly as she pushed it open and stepped inside no farther than the length of her foot. The laboratory was off-limits to her in all manners except conveying messages. The apprentices cleaned and dusted the area themselves, for fear Vita might disturb something she shouldn't. Curiosity had never come into play. She had no interest in the lab or the potions inside. There was enough work to keep her busy without having this area to worry about as well.

"Master Imrit is ready to see you off," she said, her thin voice barely reaching the ears of the students. She paused a moment before exiting, hoping for some sort of acknowledgement.

"We're on our way down," Taren said, stuffing one last bottle into his leather shoulder bag. How long would this journey take? His nerves were already getting the better of him. His mind was swirling with so many possibilities. Since leaving the cities, he had been nowhere but the Mage's College and Imrit's cottage. Heading out into the unknown was not part of the comfortable life he had hoped to lead. His plans were to master the art of herbalism and spend countless hours in a laboratory. Mixing potions and concocting new brews were his passions, unlike most students of the arcane. Still, there was much need for mages who were efficient potion crafters, and he had taken a liking to it.

The other two apprentices finished their work and headed down the stairs along with Taren. They were both more skilled than him when it came to elemental magic. Tissa had perfected the art of air magic, giving her the power to pull energy from the wind itself. Djo had studied so many years of fire magic that he thought he could solve every problem with flames. Once he nearly set the cottage ablaze, but Master Imrit had been quick to suppress the fire despite his slowing reflexes.

Unlike Tissa and Djo, Taren had spent a number of years under Master Imrit's care. Usually an apprentice would spend only the last year of study directly under a single master's instruction. Taren, however, had been unable to pay tuition and was forced to leave the Mage's College. Master Imrit saw something special in the boy, and decided to take him under his wing and continue his education free of charge. He had proved a kind and patient father figure, something Taren had never truly known. When the time came for Imrit to choose his final group of apprentices, he had chosen Tissa and Djo after carefully scrutinizing every detail of their academic records. Taren nearly fell over when Imrit announced that he himself would be Imrit's third and final apprentice. Never before had anyone been considered for an apprenticeship to a master wizard without being enrolled in the College. Taren expected to make a living as an herbalist despite his lack of a supreme title. Imrit, it seemed, had other ideas. Taren had joined Tissa and Djo in their final year of study, and was now ready to take on his final challenge.

As the trio reached the bottom of the stairs, Master Imrit's eyes twinkled with delight. "Ah," he said, "to be young again." Chuckling to himself, he turned and headed outside the cottage, the three apprentices following behind.

The sun beamed high in the east, its rays filtering down through wisps of white cloud. It was still early, and the birds clamored from their perches amid the trees. The Barrens stood foreboding only a few hundred yards from the cottage, their presence ever daunting to any who passed by. Though the trees there grew taller than anywhere in Ky'sall, there was no vegetation on the ground. No flowers, no shrubs, no plants of any kind grew in the tainted soil of The Barrens. How the trees thrived there was a mystery, even to those of magical abilities. Rumors of curses and accidents by various wizards abounded to explain the mystery of The Barrens, but none of those stories had ever been confirmed. Master Imrit enjoyed the solitude that being near such a land brought. It was rare to find travelers in the area, and he was seldom bothered by peddlers, which left him free to pursue his magical studies in peace.

Imrit led the way, dressed in his finest indigo robe with gold embellishments. For the past year, he had dazzled his students with talk of a lost symbol that held incredible power. An ancient sorceress was said to have possessed it, and her tomb was the symbol's last known location. The apprentices were tasked with retrieving it and assisting their master in unlocking its secrets. Rather than give them each a separate task to fulfill their duties as apprentices, Imrit decided it was best if all three of them worked together to find the symbol. His only regret was that he was too old to accompany them on the long and difficult journey.

"Come now, don't fall behind," Imrit said without turning around. He quickened his pace as he approached the tree line.

The apprentices followed behind, occasionally glancing at each other. Their eyes were wide, but their faces were expressionless as they attempted to suppress their anxiety. Stopping at the edge of the woods, Tissa brushed imaginary dirt away from her yellow robe. Fiddling with her light-brown hair, she awaited further instruction from her master. Her stomach felt as though a million winged creatures were trapped inside as she stared into the woods.

Djo stood tall, his chest high in an attempt to appear confident. His deep-red robe flapped slightly on the wind, adding to his kingly appearance. With his sandy-blond hair and stunning blue eyes, he already had the look of royalty. Inside, his heart was pounding, but he was determined not to show any fear. This was the final step in achieving his dream, and nothing would hold him back.

Taren's eyes glanced at each of his companions and his master in turn. He made no effort to hide his apprehension. His chest moved visibly with each breath, and he constantly tugged at the clasp of his dark-green robe. He looked everywhere except into the forest. Though he knew he would soon be inside it, he had no desire to think about it. Whatever was to come would come, but for this moment, he was standing in a familiar land that was safe and comfortable.

"At least one of you has to succeed," Imrit announced. "It will be easier if all of you can stay together, but that might not be possible. Whoever is strong enough to retrieve the symbol will have earned the rank of master. We will unlock the symbol's power together, sharing in its glory."

"One of us?" Taren asked, his voice quivering slightly. "What of the others?"

"They will likely be dead," Imrit replied, hanging his head low. "Your chances are better if you work together, and it might not be possible to complete the mission alone. I cannot say."

The three apprentices exchanged worried looks, none of them daring to say a word. They could almost read each other's minds, and each was frightened by the prospect of taking on this journey alone. Most apprentices completed their final tasks solo, thus earning the rank of master on their own. Their situation was unique, though. Master Imrit had finally discovered the symbol's location, and he would break any rule to see that it was found and placed in his care. The challenge should prove great enough for all three to qualify as masters.

"Head south through the woods until the wool looks strange, and then continue until it's normal again," Imrit declared. "One of you must succeed."

Wool? Taren wondered. *Has he lost his mind?* None of the apprentices had any idea what he meant by those words.

"It's imperative you don't use magic until you are beyond the borders of The Barrens," the elderly master added. "There is a creature living in these woods who detests its use, and it will find you should you choose to disobey. Avoid the path at all costs, and good luck to you."

Djo was the first to step forward, disappearing inside the dense trees of The Barrens. He did not look back. Taking a deep breath, Tissa followed him into the woods. Reluctantly, Taren lifted his right foot and stepped forward. Looking over his shoulder, he saw the proud smile on his master's face. It was only slightly comforting to know that Imrit believed in their abilities. Why else would he send them on such a journey? Shaking his head, Taren pushed his way between the trees, immersing himself within the strange woods.

Though the light had been bright outside the woods, inside it was dark, as if dusk had already arrived. There was no vegetation on the ground—only stray rocks and fallen limbs littered the forest floor. His two companions had stopped as well to take in their surroundings. It was obvious none of them felt comfortable, but going back would only disappoint their master.

A single north-south path ran through the forest. This path would lead them on their journey, but they had been warned not to set foot upon it. Magic was forbidden here, and the path contained traces of ancient magic from the elves who had built the road long ago. Now the path was little more than packed dirt, visible only because of the difference between its dark color and that of the yellow-brown forest floor. The ground appeared to consist of decomposing leaves that had fallen from the massive trees. The air was stale, and a claustrophobic feeling set in upon the three of them.

Taren looked back once more to say goodbye to his master, but the forest had swallowed him completely. There was no sign of Imrit or his cottage in the distance. A sense of panic came over him, but he pushed it aside, determined not to look foolish in front of the others. Still, he would be more at ease if he could at least spot the smoke rising from his master's chimney. Straining to see past the dense line of trees, he could see nothing but more forest. He felt as if he'd walked into another world entirely.

The trio silently began walking, carefully watching their steps as they went. They kept slightly right of the path, making sure not to step on it but also not to stray too far. There were no visible landmarks, and they would easily lose their way if they lost sight of the road.

None of them had skills as woodsmen, so tracking each other would be impossible if they became separated. For that reason, they remained close to one another despite having to constantly split up to maneuver around the trees.

Taren observed no visible signs of life within the woods. There was no birdsong, and there were no squirrels running up and down the massive trunks. He thought it remarkable that there were no limbs at his level, which was likely the reason no deer or other creatures could be seen. If there were any living creatures in this forest, they must exist high above the canopy. Taren paused momentarily to look upward, wondering how tall these trees must be. They rose for miles, it seemed, blotting out the sunlight above with their thick leaves.

"Don't fall behind," Djo called from ahead.

Taren hadn't realized how long he had been staring at the trees. "I'm coming," he called back, hurrying to catch up to his companions.

"We should camp here for the night," Djo said. "Darkness is falling fast."

They weren't sure if it was truly night or if it was only the lack of light making its way through the trees, but they were all feeling tired and grateful to take a rest.

"How long were we walking?" Tissa asked. Everything had looked the same as they journeyed, and her aching feet were the only sign she had moved an inch that day.

"We've gone at least twelve miles," Djo declared. He seemed certain of this even though his companions had their doubts.

"Should we build a fire?" Tissa asked.

"Yes, but not with magic," Djo replied. He scoured the immediate vicinity for fallen branches that were small enough to lift. There weren't many, but there were enough to make a small fire that would help take away the chill of night.

Taren sat back against a large fallen log. Sifting through his pack, he made note of the potions he had brought with him. Not only had he brought some concoctions to restore and energize his magical stores, he had also brought a variety of medicines in case one of them became ill. With no way of knowing which plants would be available to him, he had decided to come prepared. Once he was content he hadn't forgotten anything, he shut the bag and reclined against the log.

Tissa moved to sit next to him, pulling her knees close to her chest. "How long do you think it will be before we reach the end of The Barrens?" she asked.

"A few days at least," Taren replied. Seeing her uneasy expression, he added, "I wish we were out of here now."

Tissa nodded her agreement. She twisted at the small gold ring that she wore upon her left hand. It was a magical ring, a gift from her mother. Should she choose to use the small amount of magic it held, it would bring her comfort. Knowing that magic was forbidden here, she decided against using the ring. "It's hot in here, isn't it?" Beads of sweat had formed on her brow, and she was visibly uncomfortable.

"It does seem to be getting warmer," Taren agreed. The light was fading fast, but there was no chill to accompany it. Instead, the air seemed to be getting denser.

Djo finished building the small fire and leaned back against the trunk of a tree. "We don't need the heat, but it might keep any night creatures away." Though it was unlikely there were any creatures in these woods, the fire was a sign of home. Looking upon it gave them hope and calmed their nerves.

Finally, the trio fell asleep in the long dark of the forest. When they woke, it was still mostly dark, and they were unsure how long they had actually slept.

"We might as well get moving," Djo said as he kicked dirt over the smoldering remains of the fire.

Taren and Tissa retrieved their packs, and once again the apprentices resumed their march. The next few days went by slowly, with little conversation. Travel had proved uneventful until the fourth day. As he walked ahead of the others, Djo did not see the small branch that caught his foot. He fell hard, landing with his hands out to his sides. The fingers of his left hand brushed lightly against the path they were avoiding. Standing back on his feet, he brushed the dirt away from his robe. Taren and Tissa stared at him, wondering if he knew he had touched the path.

"I only brushed it," he said, seeing the concerned looks on their faces. Both of them had fear in their eyes, and he felt uneasy as well. Inside, he tried to convince himself that nothing would come of his misstep. "Let's get going."

Taren and Tissa continued behind him until he stopped. Coming to his side, they stopped as well.

"Did you hear something?" Djo asked.

The other two shook their heads. They stood for a moment longer, listening before continuing on their way. After a few minutes, they stopped again. This time, an unmistakable growl sounded from behind them.

In unison, they turned and saw a manlike creature, who appeared to be made of stone. He had a wide set of wings similar to the wings of a bat. Crouched low to the ground, it was clear the creature was ready to strike.

"Run!" Djo shouted.

The trio dashed through the woods, hoping to outrun the creature whose heavy footsteps pursued them. It grunted through its stone nostrils as it ran, its hot breath moving closer and closer. With a swipe of its massive clawed hand, it grabbed Djo, who had been closest to the path as they ran.

Tissa slowed for a second, but Taren grabbed her arm, forcing her to continue her flight. Without looking back, they heard the cries of their companion. There was nothing they could do. To their horror, the creature was not satisfied by taking the one who had touched the path. It continued its pursuit of the remaining two apprentices, gaining ground on them as they tired.

Taren and Tissa struggled for breath as they were forced to keep running. The trees grew denser, forcing them to dodge around the massive trunks while avoiding tripping over spent limbs. Tissa stumbled only a moment, but the creature was there to catch her. As her scream pierced the air, a shiver went down Taren's spine.

The creature continued to pursue Taren, its presence looming ever closer. *Keep running, keep running,* he told himself. If his body gave out now, he would be dead for sure. His only hope was to ignore the pain growing in the bones of his feet and the pounding of his heart in his ears. Faster and faster he pushed himself to run, but the creature continued to gain ground. Just when Taren thought he was sure to die, he burst through the tree line and into the sunlight. He had escaped The Barrens.

Chapter 2

Stumbling out of the woods, Taren no longer felt the hot breath of the stone beast on his neck. Daring to cease his flight, he turned and peered between the trees. The beast was walking away, its back turned to the apprentice. He considered a moment whether he might survive reentering the woods to see if his companions were alive. A ghastly howl filled his ears as the monster stooped next to a motionless figure draped in yellow. It was Tissa, whose blood now dripped from the beast's sharp claws. Taren turned away, unable to bear the sight before him. His stomach turned sour, and he hung his head for a long moment.

A voice startled him back to reality. "Did ye come oot o' those woods?" a surprised man asked.

Taren looked up to see a farmer dressed in patched clothing. On a rope he led a yellow goat and a black-faced sheep with a red fleece. *Strange wool.* Staring at the sheep, he could hardly believe his eyes.

"Ye didna use magic in thare, did ye?" The farmer looked Taren up and down, making note of his mage's robe and leather shoulder bag. The flap had come open on the bag, revealing rows of potions strapped neatly inside. The shocked expression still worn on the mage's face revealed that he had seen the beast that lived inside the woods.

Taren looked at the man, his eyes wide. His mind still whirling from his encounter with the monster, he found no words available to him. Though he felt the urge to look behind him once more, he resisted. He could not bear the sight of his fellow apprentice being devoured by a beast. Instead, he sat heavily on the ground, still reeling from his harrowing ordeal.

The land stretched out before him in vibrant color. No recognizable grass sprung from the ground. Instead, patches of a spongelike substance in varying colors adorned the ground. There was a noticeable lack of trees to this land, yet a walled city stood less than a mile away, its wooden buildings rising high into the sky. Farmhouses dotted the landscape in the distance, and brightly colored livestock walked the fields. They were too far for him to determine exactly what species of animal they were, but their movements reminded him of cattle.

The farmer approached Taren, who still had not managed to utter a single word. Placing a hand on the young mage's shoulder, he said, "Do ye need help, lad?" He knelt down for a closer look at the mage, who was trembling slightly. "Ye should get yerself to town," he suggested, taking Taren's arm.

Assisted by the farmer, Taren once again found his feet. He looked ahead at the town and nodded slowly. The farmer pointed toward the western side of the city.

"Town's called Rixville, and thare's a gate on the western-facin' side. Ye should get yerself some rest."

Soundlessly, Taren's feet began to move. As if in a trance, he slowly made his way to the city. The farmer watched for a few minutes as Taren walked away. Finally, he was satisfied that the young man didn't need any more help, so he led his animals away. Taren did not look back.

The city sat less than a mile from the edge of The Barrens. A wooden wall nearly eight feet in height surrounded the entire town, protecting it from dangers

Taren was unaware of. Smoke rose from a dozen chimneys, and the sounds of voices calling out filled his ears as he approached. Taren turned his feet westward and approached the gate where four guards chatted lazily with one another. Three of them were sitting, while a fourth leaned lazily against the wall.

The standing guard looked Taren over only once, his bored expression unchanging. "Have business in town do ye?" he asked.

Taren nodded. "I'm looking for an inn," he replied, not knowing where his voice came from. Everything seemed surreal since encountering the stone beast.

"Head down the main street and take the second left," the guard said. "The Wigglin' Wyrm is the third building on the right. It'll do ye fine for a drink and a rest."

Entering the town, the scent of roasting meat wafted to his nostrils. Taking in a deep breath, his stomach rumbled, begging to be filled with the sweet-smelling meal. How long had it been since he stopped to eat? He could not recall. Following his feet, he turned at the second street, which was far narrower than the main road. A man carrying planks came around from a corner, nearly bashing Taren's head with a sliding board. Noticing the movement from the

26

corner of his eye, the mage barely had time to duck. Luckily, he reacted in time, and the board narrowly missed him. Turning, he ruffled his brow at the man carrying the load.

The mustachioed man returned his gaze. "Watch where yer goin' then!" he shouted before continuing on his way.

Taren shook his head and cupped his hands over his eyes. Rubbing his face briskly, he tried to shake himself from the daze that had come over him. A hot meal and something to drink would help, he decided. This day had already proved too eventful, and he needed time to gather himself before deciding whether to move on. Master Imrit would be sorely disappointed if he returned now, assuming it was possible to return. For all he knew, the beast was still waiting for him to reenter the woods. He would have to press on, but for now, he had earned a rest.

The Wigglin' Wyrm stood only a few steps away, its wooden sign dancing on the breeze. It bore the image of a skinny golden dragon with a mug of frothy ale in its hand. The outside was in disrepair, with crooked shutters and a few shingles missing from the roof. Stepping inside, he was surprised to find it well kept. The common room was already bustling with activity, despite it still being early. Most of the men inside should have been working, but they had chosen revelry instead.

Taren found a seat at the bar as far as he could get from the other patrons. A heavy woman in a low-cut bodice approached him with a wide smile, the gap between her front teeth displaying itself as a thing of beauty.

"What'll ye have, love?" she asked.

"Whatever you have cooking will be fine," he replied. "And I'll be needing a room as well."

"Got some lovely stew," she said with a wink. "It's nice and hot. Ye can have yer choice o' rooms. Might have to double up if it gets busy, mind ye." She scurried off behind the bar, disappearing through a squeaky wooden door.

The thought of sharing a room didn't appeal to Taren. This town was unknown to him, but he was aware of the general distrust of wizards in this area. Still, there was little choice unless he was prepared to scour the town for a different inn. It would be dark in a few hours, so he resigned himself to staying put regardless of who might be joining him in his room.

The large woman returned and placed a steaming bowl in front of him. Flashing another smile, she grabbed a mug from beneath the bar and filled it with a golden liquid. "Our house ale," she stated proudly. "Best in the city."

"I'm sure it is," Taren replied. Taking a sip, he fought the urge to spit it out. The ale was thin with an overly strong taste of alcohol. Now he knew why so many people shrugged off work to visit the establishment. Bringing a spoonful of stew to his mouth, he blew on it to cool it before taking a taste. To his surprise, it was quite good. The meat tasted fresh, and the potatoes and carrots were cooked perfectly. The slice of bread that accompanied it was still warm from the oven. It was flavorful and reminded him of the bread Vita would occasionally bake. He missed his home already.

Finishing his meal, he asked the woman, "How much do I owe you?"

"Ten coppers fer the room and two fer the food," she replied. "But ye won't be ready fer bed yet. Thare's a lute player comin' in a bit."

Taren wasn't in much of a mood for a party. Though he was feeling better after his meal, he still planned to retire early and get a good night's sleep before deciding what to do in the morning. Fishing in his bag, he produced the coppers and laid them on the counter. "I thought I might get to bed early," he said.

The barmaid came around to his side of the bar and pressed herself against him. "Ye sure?" she asked with a grin. "Ye'll have more fun here. Young men like ye need to have a little fun." She nudged at him with her elbow, her eyes twinkling.

Nearly forgetting to breathe, he squeaked out, "Not tonight." Quickly, he rose to his feet and pushed his stool back toward the bar before bolting up the stairs. The woman's laughter filled the air as she watched him frantically escape to safety. Apparently she was just toying with him, but his lack of experience with women had left him panicked and red in the face.

Taren ducked into the first room at the top of the stairs. It was small with few furnishings: two small beds spaced about a foot apart, a wooden table with a single chair, and one tiny square window looking out over the city. A pitcher of water and a washing bowl sat upon the table, and Taren was glad to wash the dirt away from his face. After scrubbing at his skin, he ran his wet fingers through his shaggy brown hair. He stared at his reflection a moment in the bowl, staring into his own deep brown eyes and wishing he could wash away the sights he had seen earlier in the day.

With a sigh, he removed his leather boots and lay back on the bed near the window. Placing one arm behind his head, he stared up at the ceiling and waited for sleep to find him. After a few moments, he crossed his arms over his chest and closed his eyes. Still, sleep eluded him. He tossed a few times, finally ending up on his right side. Drifting off to sleep, he dreamed he was back in The Barrens, with the other apprentices at his side. This time, it was him who touched the path, standing upon it with both feet as his two companions watched in horror. The stone beast appeared before him, slashing at his face before he had time to react. He awoke with a start, sitting straight up on his bed.

Thunderous applause erupted from below as the celebration continued into the night. Looking out of the window, Taren could see that night had fallen, a million stars filling the sky. Rubbing at his temples, he hoped to shake off the disturbing image of his dream, but he was too shaken. Stumbling in the darkness for his boots, he slipped them onto his feet and headed back downstairs to join the crowd. The raucous noise coming from the common room would not have allowed him to return to sleep anyway.

It had to be near midnight, and the common room was packed with people. Not only had a lute player taken to the stage, but a drummer had set up as well. Together they played a variety of songs, happily taking requests from the boisterous crowd. Taren shuffled to a table in the corner, leaning his head heavily on his hand. A server approached him, but he waved the girl away. He wasn't interested in any more of the house ale.

After sitting through a few songs, he felt even more awake than before. It was unlikely he would get any sleep this night. An uneasy feeling came over him as he realized that a figure at the opposite end of his table was staring at him. The man was dressed in dark-brown leather with a cowl covering the majority of his face. His eyes, however, were completely exposed, glowing in the dimly lit room. They were yellow like a cat's, with wide slits for pupils. Clearly, this person was not human, but Taren had never heard of such a race. Such creatures must live far from the land of Ky'sall.

Taren found himself staring back at the man, who finally stood and marched toward the young wizard. Taren tried to look away, hoping the man would walk past him, but no such luck. The yellow-eyed man took a seat next to Taren, setting his mug down on the table.

"You seem out of sorts," the man said in a raspy voice. He brushed back his cowl, allowing Taren a clear view of his face. His blue-green skin was scaly, obviously reptilian. His snakelike head featured rows of spikes on either side, his nose little more than two nostril slits above his mouth. "I'm not from around here either," he added.

Taren stared a moment, not sure how to respond. Never in his life had he encountered another of this man's race. "I'm from Dobra," Taren admitted. Though he had been born in a farming village, he had spent a few years at the Mage's College in Dobra before moving to its outskirts to live with Master Imrit. It was as good a hometown as any.

The reptile man nodded. "You're a mage," he said. "We don't get many of those around here." He sipped at his drink, waiting for Taren to continue the conversation.

Taren wasn't sure what to say. What was this man's interest in him? Was he just being friendly or was there some ulterior motive? "Yes, I'm a mage," he finally said. "My name is Taren."

The man smiled, turning up the corners of his wide, scaly mouth. "My name's Zamna," he said. "I'm an assassin."

Taren was slightly taken aback by the man's sudden announcement of his profession. "Why would someone hire you to kill me?" he asked out loud. Instantly, he regretted allowing the words to leave his mouth.

Zamna laughed a strange hissing laugh. "If I'd wanted to kill you, you would be dead. I don't converse with my targets."

Taren's tense posture relaxed a bit. Clearly this man was an undesirable. Taren hadn't noticed, but when Zamna moved closer to him, the table nearest to him cleared out, each person slowly vacating his seat, one after the other. "Then what do you want with me?"

"You look like someone who has a mission to accomplish. This town gets a handful of travelers each year, but none of them are wizards. Something has drawn you this way, and I thought you might be in need of a little assistance. I occasionally provide services as a bodyguard, and I know this land fairly well."

Taren grew suspicious. "How do you know about my mission?"

"I don't," Zamna admitted. "A troubled young man who keeps to himself in a roomful of merrymaking must have a lot on his mind. Perhaps a task of some importance weighs heavily on you."

Taren admired the reptile man's ability to read him. The idea of completing his mission alone was indeed troubling. Imrit had intended for all three apprentices to work together to retrieve the symbol. Alone, Taren stood little chance. But how could he trust an assassin? This man probably intended to rob him and kill him once they were away from witnesses. "Why would you offer me your assistance?" Taren asked. He crossed his arms and tried his best to look intimidating.

"Money," Zamna replied casually. "A wizard's quest no doubt involves treasure," he added. "I'd be happy to have a share of it. You are heading someplace dangerous and are in need of a little protection. I happen to be quite handy with these daggers." He pulled a shining silver dagger from its sheath on his chest and a second from an unseen holster on his hip. Twirling them once, he laid them on the table and grinned at the young mage. "I have quite a reputation around here for fighting, but you'll notice I have no scars upon my scales. What do you say?"

Taren's mind flashed back to the stone beast. Could Zamna have defeated it? Swallowing hard, Taren came to a decision. He would tell this man where he was heading and judge by his reaction whether he was worth employing. After all, Imrit had not sworn any of them to secrecy. Only a mage could claim the symbol. "I am heading to the tomb of the ancient sorceress Ailwen."

Zamna laughed again, this time tossing his head back. Noticing that Taren had not cracked a smile, he stopped and asked, "You're serious?"

A single nod was Taren's only reply.

"It lies far to the south, through forests, deserts, and swamps," Zamna stated. "That is no mission to undertake alone."

"You know the way?" Taren asked, not revealing that he had a map in his bag. He was certain he could find the way on his own, but surviving to that point might prove difficult. After all, he was an herbalist, not a battle mage. Had Tissa and Djo been free to perform magic, he was certain they would have taken down the stone beast. Unfortunately, casting magic in The Barrens could have summoned more beasts to overwhelm them. Now alone, he had no one to provide protection from whatever he might encounter along the way. Though he was far from defenseless, he was less than confident in his fighting abilities.

"I've never been that far south," Zamna admitted. "But I do know the land south of here, and I've survived a desert before."

"What payment are you demanding?" Taren asked.

"A portion of whatever's in that tomb," Zamna replied. "I doubt anyone has disturbed it, seeing as it's cursed." He shrugged as he said those last words, obviously unbothered by such a minor detail.

"We'll leave at first light," Taren declared, hoping he had made the right decision. With an ally, he would be more likely to survive the road ahead. At least now he stood a chance of success. If it became necessary to defend himself against his own companion, he hoped his magic would prove strong enough to best the reptilian man, or at least give him time to escape.

Zamna re-sheathed his daggers and lifted his mug. After taking a long swig, he reached forward to shake Taren's hand. "Don't worry," he said. "I never kill anyone who owes me money." Grinning, he added, "But I make no promises after I'm paid."

Chapter 3

The next morning, Taren awoke with regrets.

Holding his head in his hands, he sat up on his bed, scolding himself. How could he have agreed to allow an assassin to accompany him on the most important journey of his life? Master Imrit had placed his trust in Taren, and now he had risked losing everything. This reptile man could probably kill him faster than he could cast a defensive spell.

Gathering his thoughts, he decided to tell Zamna there had been a change in plans. He would admit that he hadn't been thinking clearly since his ordeal earlier, and he had made a mistake. Now that he'd had time to gather his thoughts, he knew this was a journey he would have to undertake alone. But how could he tell a killer that he'd changed his mind? This man was expecting payment in the form of treasure. Taren couldn't possibly provide that. He made up his mind to sneak out quietly, avoiding the situation altogether. With luck, Zamna would not consider him worth tracking down.

Taren rose from the bed and quickly collected his few belongings. Opening the door quietly, he tiptoed into the hallway and down the stairs. If only there were a back door to the establishment, he wouldn't have to pass through the common room. Zamna might be sitting there waiting to leave. To Taren's relief, only a few men sat around eating breakfast. The reptilian man was nowhere to be seen. Perhaps he had changed his mind and decided against spending miserable days crossing a desert. There was a good chance someone had plundered the tomb in ages past, so there was no real reason for Zamna to come along. Except, of course, that he was familiar with the area and might not be bad to have around in a fight. Taren shook the thought away. No, he would travel alone and retrieve the symbol unassisted.

Stepping out into the sunlight, Taren breathed the fresh air deep into his lungs. He closed his eyes and turned his face to the sun, momentarily basking in its warm embrace. Out of nowhere, something crashed into his midsection. Opening his eyes, he stood face to face with Zamna, who was once again hooded. Taren's mouth dropped open, but no sound came out.

"You'll be needing that bedroll," Zamna said, still holding it against the mage's torso. "The sand will be uncomfortable if it gets between your scales," he added, hissing with laughter.

Taking the pack, Taren slung it over his back. "Thanks," he muttered. It would add weight to the bundle he was already carrying, but it would provide more padding than the thin blanket he had brought.

"We should get a few more supplies," Zamna said. "You'll need more water than me, and we don't want to run low on food. We might need to pick up some medicine as well, just in case."

"I can handle that myself," Taren informed him. "I'm an herbalist." Unlatching his shoulder bag, he held it open for Zamna to look inside.

The assassin nodded his approval. "Let's get some food then."

Stepping down from the inn stairs, Taren said, "Look, this really is something I should do alone. You don't need to come along." He couldn't dare say what he was really thinking. He did not trust this person, and he'd been an idiot to invite him along.

Zamna narrowed his eyes. "You'll never make it alone," he said. "The only reason you got away from the stone beast was because the other two were slower than you."

Taren stared at him in disbelief. Had he revealed more than he meant to last night? His memory was blurry, and he could not recollect when he had returned to bed. Perhaps he had partaken of too much house ale, despite promising himself he would have no more of it. The mage vaguely remembered the reptile man insisting they drink on their agreement. What had he told this man about the symbol? Revealing too much might put him in danger. This assassin could easily take it from him once he'd retrieved it. It was possible he was a mage as well and was hiding it.

"Ailwen's tomb is rumored to be full of riches," Zamna said, filling the silence. "Now that you've put the idea in my head, I'm going, and I'll need a mage to open the door."

"Why is that?" Taren wondered.

"Because it's sealed with magic," Zamna replied, shaking his head. "Do you know nothing of the place you're going?"

"I know a little," Taren replied, trying to hold his head high. In reality, little was known of the tomb.

Master Imrit had studied more than anyone else on the subject, and he had little information to pass on. Once he had discovered its location, he had mapped out the route that his apprentices should take and left it at that. How to get inside and retrieve the symbol was up to the them. With the three of them together, surely they could figure it out. Imrit had grown old and impatient, and his apprentices were eager to please. They had convinced themselves they could do anything. Never once had they imagined not making it out of The Barrens.

The other apprentices were gone, fallen at the hands of a monster. Taking in a deep breath, Taren resolved to complete his quest, and return with the symbol or die trying. What harm could there be in allowing Zamna to join him? Two heads were better than one, weren't they? Letting out the breath slowly, Taren said, "Let's get what we need and be on our way." His chances of success seemed good, as long as Zamna proved to be a man of his word. If he wasn't, Taren would probably find out sooner rather than later. After all, if he intended only to rob him and kill him, he would probably do it as soon as they left town. Taren decided he would take the risk. Alone in the wilderness, he would likely die anyway.

Together they walked down the narrow street leading into the main thoroughfare. Market stalls lined each side of the wide road, and numerous vendors called out in loud voices in hopes of attracting customers. Taren's eye fell on a baker's stall, where sticky sweet rolls displayed themselves with pride, begging him to indulge. Resisting the urge, he pressed on. This was not the time to satiate his sweet tooth. Provisions needed to be kept light for the long journey ahead. Walking all day with a heavy pastry in his stomach would only lead to problems.

Though Taren had brought some rations from Imrit's cottage, he had no idea how long the journey would take. It couldn't hurt to purchase more while he had the chance. The pair stopped at a stall where nuts and dried fruit were stocked in abundance. A thin man with a gaunt face smiled at them from behind the counter.

"What'll ye have?" he asked.

"Do you have any dried meat?" Taren asked, hoping the local cuisine was not too different from what he was used to.

"Aye," the man replied. "We got beef strips and crickers."

Taren paused a moment, wondering if he should ask what crickers were. "Two pounds of beef for me," he said, before looking over at Zamna.

"A pound of crickers," Zamna said. "We also need three pounds of dry fruit and four pounds of nuts. You can mix a variety together."

With a nod, the man began filling thick paper pouches with the requested provisions.

"Do you think that will be enough?" Taren asked.

"There will be more along the way," Zamna promised. "I know what's edible out there."

Taren nodded, glad to have his companion's knowledge of the area. The young apprentice had a good knowledge of plants, so he doubted he would accidentally ingest anything poisonous, but he wasn't sure what he would find in this strange land. Of course, what was poisonous to him might not be to someone of Zamna's race. Taren had no idea.

The merchant handed over the bags to Zamna, who shoved them inside his pack. With his hand out, the man stared at Taren. Rummaging in his sack, Taren pulled out a few copper coins.

"Is this enough?" he asked.

The man nodded. "Good day to ye."

"What are crickers?" Taren asked as the pair headed back to the road.

"Dried crickets," Zamna replied. "Good source of protein."

Taren felt himself start to gag, but he swallowed hard to fight it. Zamna could keep the entire bag of crickers for himself.

As they approached the city gate, they stepped aside to allow a few farmers to enter with their carts. The bright-blue fur of the mules hauling the wares into town caught Taren's eye. They were much more impressive than the brownish-red mules he was used to seeing. They trotted along the road, bringing a splash of color to an otherwise drab city.

"We're leaving just in time," Zamna commented. "It's market day."

Taren wouldn't mind taking a look at the colorful wares in the cart, but he knew there was no time to waste. The sooner he could get going, the sooner he could find the symbol and return to his master. With a final look, he said goodbye to the city of Rixville. He hoped to be passing this way again soon, when it was time to return home.

Stepping outside the gate, a system of well-worn roads spread out before them. Those running east-west had seen the most travel, as evidenced by the deep ruts cut into them. The road leading south was less worn, but it was clearly visible. The landscape was dotted with houses and farms of varying size, but there was little to be seen close to the road. The land was mostly flat and covered in the spongy, bright-colored grass Taren had noticed before.

Choosing the south-leading path, they marched side by side in silence while Taren took in the sights of the area. Zamna kept his eyes forward, carefully watching the way ahead. He moved in a businesslike manner, his head occasionally glancing to the side. After a few miles, Taren could bear the silence no longer.

"How long do you think it will take to reach the tomb?" he asked.

"Hard to say," Zamna replied. "A few weeks at least, assuming the land is traversable and we don't have to go out of our way." He kept his gaze forward as he spoke.

"Are you originally from Rixville?" Taren asked, in an effort to prolong the conversation.

"No," he snorted, shaking his head. Clearly he thought the question was daft.

"Then where are you from?" Taren wondered aloud. Zamna was the first he had seen of a reptilian race, and he'd never read about them in his studies.

Dropping his head, Zamna sighed. He disliked being interrogated, and he had no intention of sharing much with this young wizard. However, in order to satiate his curiosity, Zamna was willing to answer this one question. "I come from a land far across the sea. It is known as La'kerta."

Taren raised his eyebrows, hoping to find out more about the reptilian homeland. "So you're La'kertan then," he said.

"Yes, Ky'sallan," Zamna snapped, clearly agitated.

Taren decided not to press his companion any further. Perhaps as they traveled he would open up more and allow Taren to know him better. For now, the mage pictured a land crawling with reptiles, some of them on two legs, others on four. Did they crawl out of the sea in some pre-larval stage like a salamander? Looking at his companion's scales, he decided he couldn't be any type of amphibian. His skin was too dry. Still, he wondered if he might have hatched from an egg. Keeping his mouth tightly shut, he held back the question for a later time.

The road stretched on as they continued their march away from the city. The walls grew farther away until nothing could be seen of Rixville. Farms came and went, and Taren finally got a better look at the animals he had seen from a distance. They were indeed cattle, as he had suspected earlier, and they came in a wide assortment of colors. Some of them were solid, but the majority were dappled with a multitude of hues. One in particular stood out to him, as it had a bright-green head and brown and white splotches on its back. It reminded him of the ducks that used to inhabit the small pond outside his dormitory window. This land was a far cry from the Mage's College grounds.

One farm spread wide enough that it nearly touched the road. Taren instantly recognized some of the herbs growing in neat rows just behind a wooden fence. Straying from the road, the mage dared to approach the fence.

"I wouldn't do that," Zamna warned. "Those go for a lot of money, and the farmer won't take kindly to a thief, even a magical one."

Taren halted in his tracks. He had no wish to antagonize anyone, but he regretted the scarcity of ingredients in this land. "Why are there no wild plants in this region?"

"Nothing grows wild anymore," Zamna replied. "It's been that way for centuries. Every tree, every plant, every bit of food comes from those farms. Eventually we'll reach the woods, and you'll see all the plants you could desire." His tone sounded almost bored.

Stepping back onto the road, Taren resumed his march. "I've brought quite a variety of potions, but it couldn't hurt to harvest more ingredients while I travel," he stated. "You never know what we might need."

"So that's what's weighing you down," Zamna remarked, pointing at Taren's shoulder bag. "You brought more than you needed. The first rule of the road is to travel light."

"There are a few more sewn into pockets in my robe," Taren said with a smile. Undoing a small toggle, he opened a flap on the hip of his robe to reveal five small vials.

"Let me guess," Zamna said. "Those are the most important."

Taren shrugged. "Depends on the situation. Some of those will replenish my magical stores should I become depleted."

Wrinkling his brow, Zamna asked, "Don't you regenerate that naturally?"

"No," Taren replied. "Elves do, but we humans have to rely on potions. We also have a harder time learning magic. For a time, I wished I had been born an elf." He laughed softly, remember his childhood fantasy of being a tall, blond-haired elf.

"How do they taste?" Zamna asked.

"The potions? They're not too bad. I craft my own, and I usually add a drop of honey or fruit juice to contrast the bitterness."

"I don't know how much of that we'll be finding," Zamna remarked.

They continued until sunset, when Zamna finally suggested they take a rest. Taren was grateful for the opportunity to sit, and his stomach had been rumbling for hours.

"Is there anywhere to find cover?" Taren asked.

"Cover from what?" Zamna sounded puzzled.

"Rain, animals, anything," Taren replied. "It seems strange to sleep out in the open."

"Used to feather beds are you?" the La'kertan hissed. "You'll be all right. It doesn't rain here, and there are no wild animals this close to the farms."

Taren almost accepted this explanation, but he could not. "If it doesn't rain, how do the farms stay fertile?"

"Magic," Zamna replied. "I'd think a mage could recognize it."

Taren felt embarrassed. He had no ability to sense whether another person practiced magic. Again, he wondered what it must be like to be an elf and have that ability. Could Zamna sense the magic? "Are you capable of magic?" he asked.

"Capable?" Zamna echoed. "Perhaps. I've never tried." With those words, he unrolled his bed and sat down cross-legged.

"Should we build a fire?" Taren wondered. He had no idea if it would be cold at night. Another thing he had not prepared for. If he used magic to warm himself, he would become depleted too fast. If only he had mastered the element of fire.

"Not necessary," Zamna said. "The temperature stays constant."

Relieved, Taren unrolled his bed as well and sat across from his companion. Zamna reached inside his pack to retrieve the provisions they had bought earlier that day. Offering them to Taren, the mage gladly took the strips of beef and some fruit. Zamna was content to keep the crickers to himself, and he lazily popped them into his mouth as he reclined on his arm.

"Tell me," Zamna began. "How did you come to be a magical human?"

The sudden interest in his life took Taren by surprise. Zamna's tone was sincere, almost friendly. Taren may have been too hasty in fearing him, as it seemed the reptilian man had no interest in killing him.

"I was the third son of nine children born to a yeoman, or so I was told. My family was poor, and I stood to inherit nothing. Luckily, I exhibited a spark of talent for magic when I was just learning to walk. I was taken into basic mage training."

"Who took you?" Zamna inquired.

"The Red Council makes it a point to visit all children in Ky'sall to determine whether they have magical inclinations. If so, they are taken for training. Many are sent home after a year or two. I was lucky."

"How so?" Zamna asked as he popped another cricker in his mouth.

"I had enough magical aptitude to be allowed to continue my training. Unfortunately, my parents were expected to pay for my tuition, as often happens. They couldn't afford it. My sisters needed dowries, and I was a burden."

Zamna leaned up on his arm to look at the apprentice. "But you obviously found a way to continue your training." Lifting a hand, he gestured to Taren's robe and bag full of potions.

"My master, Imrit, took a liking to me. He saw potential and encouraged me to work hard. The Red Council would have sent me to work as a house servant if Imrit hadn't taken me into his own home and allowed me to study alongside his older apprentices."

Zamna lay back to stare up at the stars. "How nice," he said, sounding only half interested. "What then?"

"I studied day and night," he replied. "I took a liking to herbalism, and I put all my energy into it."

Zamna scoffed. "Why not learn to cast lightning or something impressive? I can't imagine anything more boring than cooking potions all day."

Taren did his best not to become offended. How could this man possibly know the intricacies of potion crafting? It was possibly the most sought-after profession among mages. Few had the skills necessary to concoct mixtures that worked correctly. "I do have basic knowledge of the elements," Taren explained. "I can cast many different types of spells, but I can master only one craft. I have chosen herbalism." He felt pride as he spoke. Truly, crafting magical elixirs was his passion. Mastering an element had its appeals, but a human could hope to master only one arcane subject in a lifetime. It was far too taxing to focus on several at once. Taren was content with his lot.

Zamna shrugged. "Suit yourself, I suppose." Rolling onto his side, he turned away from the mage and closed his eyes.

Taren sat up a while longer before finally lying back on his bed. The stars were dim overhead, despite the obvious lack of clouds. The night sky had a purple hue to it, with splashes of pale pink mixed in. He wondered how this land had become so colorful, but the snoring of his companion let him know there was no use asking. Deep down, he already knew the answer: magic.

Chapter 4

After days of marching southward, Taren felt as though an eternity had passed. There had been little conversation so far, and no interesting sights to observe along the way. Finally the land began to change. Sparse patches of green grass sprouted in random spots along the road, and a few small trees stood in the distance. Taren felt relief to see the terrain becoming more like his home. Only one remaining farmhouse with its multicolored livestock could be seen far from the road. Taking one last look back, Taren bid farewell to the strange, colorful land.

"Something has been bothering me," Zamna said, breaking the long silence that had existed between the two travelers.

Taren, startled by his companion's sudden desire for talk, asked, "What is that?"

Zamna paused in his walking and turned to face the mage. "You said your parents couldn't pay for your education. I don't understand why this Red Council would take you away and then expect someone else to pay for it. If they wanted to train you, they should have done so regardless of payment."

Taren was surprised that the La'kertan would point out the injustice of his situation. A man who kills for money surely looks out only for himself. Perhaps Taren had misjudged him. "It isn't right, is it?" he replied. "It's their way of weeding out the poor and giving the rich, noble families the opportunity to get ahead. There are very few mages who aren't from prominent families."

Shaking his head, Zamna commented, "The ruling elite. It's the same in my homeland, only worse."

"How so?" Taren wondered.

"There are many factions who desire power," Zamna explained. "You join one, and the others are ready to hunt you down." Having said all he was willing to reveal, he resumed his course along the road.

Though it hadn't lasted long, Taren was grateful for the momentary pause. His feet were not used to so much walking, and occasionally he had a hard time keeping up with his companion. The La'kertan had a fluid, silent motion about him, and he moved with ease over the flat terrain. Taren suspected he would move well through any environment, and he wondered what the reptilian homeland must be like. The question would have to wait for another day. Zamna was not forthcoming with personal information, and Taren had no desire to risk angering his companion with questions.

The trees became less scarce as they moved along the road. The ground now appeared completely green, with no sign of the strange grass that surrounded Rixville. The land before them was wide, with tall grass and long stocks bearing fluffy-white tufts at the top. An occasional yellow flower reached high, its face shining high above the grass. Most of the trees were saplings, but there were a number of them to be seen, some of them coming close to the edge of the road. The air seemed fresher, and Taren breathed it deeply into his lungs. He felt more at home than he had the past few days.

A high-pitched squeal broke through the air, startling Taren from his reverie. Zamna instinctively drew his daggers and crouched low to the ground.

Taren knelt down next to him, hoping his companion would know what had made the sound and whether it was a threat to them.

Zamna brought a finger to his lips, instructing the mage to remain silent. Taren clamped his mouth shut, only then realizing that it was hanging open. The squeal pierced the silence once again, followed by a loud snort. After a moment, footsteps pawed at the ground. A smile stretched across the La'kertan's face. Taren did not understand.

"A spiny hog," Zamna whispered, licking his lips.

Nodding that he understood, Taren stood cautiously. Spiny hogs could be rather nasty, and the males were terribly aggressive. It stood under a tree, looking the same as the feral hogs he had seen in Ky'sall with its wiry, red-brown hair and a single row of black spines running in a ridge along its back. Taren made note of its tusks curling up from its mouth to its snout.

"A male," he whispered, "about twenty yards away near that tree." He gestured his thumb in the direction of the hog.

With a single nod, Zamna crept forward into the grass, disappearing from view. Taren stayed put, wondering if he should follow. He'd never actually hunted an animal before, but he hated to stand still while his companion did all the work. He would be sharing in the reward of a fresh dinner, and it didn't seem right to stand idle.

Looking in the direction of the hog, he could see no sign of Zamna. Then, the hog suddenly turned and sniffed the air. *It must be aware of Zamna's presence,* he thought. Cracking his knuckles, he bent low and extended his hands toward the hog. Muttering an incantation under his breath, he focused his energy at the creature. A single beam of green magic cracked through the air, extending from his hand to the hog. Missing the animal by only inches, it hopped in the air and turned its attention to Taren. Before the mage could chide himself for his mistake, Zamna leapt forward from the grass, his dagger finding its target in the hog's neck. It hung lifelessly in his arms, never knowing what had taken its life.

Taren made his way to his companion, while Zamna immediately set to work gutting the animal. The sight was gruesome but not unbearable. If they were going to have fresh meat, something had to die. Taren searched the ground for fallen branches to start a fire. If he couldn't assist in catching dinner, the least he could do was help cook it. Finding a suitable amount of wood, he trampled the grass and fashioned a ring of stones to contain the flames. Arranging the wood in a neat pile, he extended a hand and shot red magic into the center. A fire roared to life.

"Got it on the first try," Zamna jibed, hissing softly with laughter. "What were you trying to do anyway? Blow it up?"

"Had it worked, it would have paralyzed the creature, making it easier to catch," Taren explained.

"Well, at least you distracted it, I guess," Zamna replied. "It's easy to sneak up on a person, but an animal can smell you coming. I'm glad I didn't have to wrestle with this one." He lifted the head of the hog and presented it to Taren, who was already fashioning a spit. The mage took it with a smile and placed it over the fire to cook.

Though the meat was a little tough, having something fresh was a welcome change from strips of dried beef. Taren ate his fill plus a few extra bites. Zamna seemed to enjoy the meat as well, as he devoured a large portion of the hog's hind quarter before stopping to take a breath.

His stomach feeling ready to burst, Taren rummaged around in his pack for a solution. Finding a bundle of Golden Thread leaves, he pulled two of them out and placed one in his mouth. It had a slight tanginess to it, which was not unwelcome after a meal of so much meat. Extending his hand, he offered the second leaf to Zamna. "It will help with stomach upset," he declared. "Also, it will fight any bacteria that might not have cooked away. You can't be too careful with these unfamiliar food sources."

Zamna hesitated for a moment, looking at the leaf. Slowly he reached for it and turned it over in his hand. With a shrug, he placed it in his mouth and chewed. His eyes squinted as the sourness hit him, and he resisted the urge to spit it out. The aftertaste was tolerable, but he wouldn't be so quick to take medicine from his companion the next time. Reaching into what was left of the hog's carcass, he found a suitably small bone. Reclining against the base of the tree, he picked at his pointed teeth. With a supportive hand on his midsection, he let out a sizable burp. "I think we're done for the day," he commented.

Taren nodded. His legs and feet were aching, and walking on a full stomach would only add to his discomfort.

"Tell me, mage," Zamna began, "what lies inside Ailwen's tomb that is of importance to you?"

Taren hesitated in his answer. Zamna had said the tomb's door was sealed with magic, and only a mage would be able to get inside. The La'kertan had come along for the treasure, and it was possible he intended to take everything—including the symbol. Would this man kill him once they had retrieved it? Being nonmagical, he couldn't hope to use it for himself, but it was probably worth a fortune to the right buyer. Did anyone know the symbol's true potential besides Imrit? Maybe it was safe to talk to Zamna, but Taren wasn't sure.

The symbol had been lost for centuries, and there was no talk of the sorceress Ailwen anymore. Taren and the other apprentices had never heard of her when their master first described her immense power. No book at the Mage's College had recorded anything about her life. It was as if she never existed. It was doubtful other mages had studied her as closely as Imrit. His interests were quite different from those of his peers, and he had often been ridiculed because of it. It was possible that this quest was in vain, and no such item actually existed. It was also possible that the item had been destroyed, or that the tomb had already been plundered. Some thief might have sold the symbol for its value in precious metals, never knowing its true potential.

"Is your mission so secret?" Zamna wondered. With a shrug, he continued to pick at his teeth. If the mage did not wish to tell him, he would not force him. Zamna was sure there would be plenty of other treasures beside the one his companion sought. He doubted Taren was out to double-cross him. The young man had tried to ask Zamna to stay behind, whether it was because he feared him or because there was some danger ahead mattered not. Zamna was a man of his word. He would help this man in his journey, and hopefully be much richer for it. His days as a hired knife might soon be at an end.

"I seek to retrieve an item for my master, one that is rumored to be buried inside Ailwen's tomb," Taren explained. He had no desire to keep Zamna in the dark, but he wasn't sure how much was safe to tell. Imrit had not instructed the apprentices to keep the matter secret, but he might have thought it went without saying. He expected them to rely on each other, but surely he knew they might encounter others along the way. What if they needed help from an outside source? Imrit had never mentioned such a scenario.

"A magical item, no doubt," Zamna replied with renewed interest. "Why does your master not travel with you?"

"He is too old," Taren replied. "He couldn't possibly make the journey. This is my final test before I achieve the rank of master."

"You need to prove you can face peril?" Zamna asked, chuckling slightly.

"I suppose that's part of it," he said, slightly offended. Obviously, his companion had no idea what it meant to become a master of the arcane. It was everything to Taren. Making Imrit proud mattered more to him than anything else in the world.

"Am I allowed to know more about this item?" Zamna asked. "Or is it some deep dark secret that only mages can understand?" He paused a moment and added, "You might at least say what it looks like. I wouldn't want you to overlook it among the other items in the tomb."

Taren's heart nearly stopped for a moment. He had no idea what the symbol actually looked like. Imrit had never described it. It was possible the old man did not know. There were only a few surviving accounts of the symbol, and those were in decaying tomes. How would Taren know when he came across it? Was this part of the test? Surely Imrit would not have sent his apprentices on a quest if he didn't believe they could succeed. There had to be a way to know for sure when he came upon the symbol. *When I'm in its presence, I will know it,* he tried to convince himself. Though he could not shake off all doubt, he decided to trust that his master had given him all the necessary information.

Zamna shook his head. "Fine," he said. "Just one more question. If this magical item is so precious, why would you want to return it to your master? Why not keep it for yourself instead?"

"Because my master requests it," Taren replied. "He is the only father I've ever known, and I'm loyal to him." Taren looked at the ground. "I couldn't live with myself if I betrayed him." In his mind, he thought of the symbol's alleged ability to grant its wielder eternal life. His master was aging, and he did not want to lose him. He would gladly hand it over in hopes that Imrit would be around for many long years, still passing on his wisdom to Taren. Without thinking, he asked, "Do assassins know much of loyalty and honor?"

Zamna sat forward and threw his toothpick into the fire. "If I take a job, I complete it. Is that not loyalty? Am I not a man of my word?" He shook his head.

"I didn't mean—" Taren started to say.

"Believe it or not, there are people in this world who deserve to be killed," Zamna spat. "Don't judge me with your high-and-mighty attitude. Your people sell young children into slavery. Would it not be appropriate to kill an owner who treats his slave badly?"

"I…I don't know," Taren replied, stumbling on his words.

"Trust me, mage, people like me are doing you a favor. You live your sugar-coated life and believe that everything works out in the end. I'm one of those people making sure that things do, in fact, work out for the better."

Taren regretted his words and wished he could take them back. His companion had clearly been offended, and that was not his intention. For the last few days, he felt they were becoming friends, and he hated the thought of losing that. "Forgive me," he said. "I didn't mean to disparage you or your profession. And you're right. I have led a sheltered life. I know very little of things outside my books."

"When I make a promise to a man, I keep it," Zamna said, the anger draining from his voice.

"Others might look down on me because of my profession, but I am an honorable man."

"I believe you," Taren stated. "I apologize."

Zamna waved his hand dismissively and leaned back against the tree. Hissing with laughter, he said, "You probably thought I'd cut your throat and rob you once we were outside town."

Taren forced himself to laugh as well, hoping it didn't sound too contrived. He would never admit how he had truly perceived his companion at first.

"Believe it or not, you're worth more to me alive," Zamna said. "If that tomb holds riches, then this journey will be worth the trouble a hundred times over."

"Do you know someone who has been there?" Taren asked.

"No," Zamna replied. "And that's why it must hold treasure. If anyone in my circle had plundered it, there would be tales spoken for generations. In my travels, I've heard only that the tomb exists, and that it's impossible to get inside if you can't perform great feats of magic. I guess that means a master of the arcane has to open the door." He grinned at his companion.

"I'm not a master," he reminded him.

"True," Zamna stated. "But you will be soon. Who knows? Maybe your master made up the part about an item. Maybe your real test is to open the door."

"If that's the case, we might be in trouble."

"How so?" Zamna sat forward once again.

"Well, my master sent three of us to find the tomb. Maybe we need three mages who have mastered different elements in order to get inside." The prospect was daunting. How would he ever find more mages along the way?

"Let's hope that isn't the case," Zamna hissed. "I'd hate to walk all that way for nothing."

"Do you think we will come across other mages?"

"No idea," the La'kertan replied. "I suppose anything is possible. We'll just have to keep our eyes open for them." After a pause, he asked, "What element does an herbalist master?"

"Earth," Taren replied. "Though there are different ways to go with earth magic. In truth, there are different courses to pursue with all the elements. So even if we found more mages, it would be impossible to know if they had the correct skills to gain entrance to the tomb."

"I suppose they'd need the same skills as your former companions," Zamna said. "I wonder if your master knew only one of you would make it. I've never heard that a team of wizards would be required to open the door. I've only been told that it takes a master. I'll put my faith in your skills." As he finished speaking, he laid out his bedroll and stretched himself onto it.

Taren remained sitting, staring into the fire. Maybe Zamna was right, and his true test was to open the door. Imrit would probably grant him the title of master if he returned able to prove he'd been inside. The symbol had to exist, though. Master Imrit had spoken of it with fire in his eyes. Taren was determined to search every corner of that tomb until he found it, even if it took decades. He would not return to his master empty-handed.

Chapter 5

Morning brought a bright sky and soft white clouds drifting overhead. Both men were up early, their energy restored by last night's feast. Though Zamna seemed to have calmed by the time he went to sleep, Taren worried there might still be contention between them.

"I didn't mean to insult you last night," he said as he slung his bedroll over his shoulder.

"Forget it," Zamna replied without looking up.

"No hard feelings?" Taren pressed.

Zamna looked at him quizzically. "Hard feelings?"

"It's an expression," Taren explained.

Zamna grunted. Rising to his feet, he said, "Let's get moving."

As far as Taren could tell, that was Zamna's way of saying he was forgiven. In the future, he would be more guarded with his words. This man had so far proved a fine companion, and he was willing to face whatever dangers might await them.

With the wind at their backs, the pair set off to continue their journey south. As they pressed on, the trees became more numerous, and the terrain became rougher. Rocks and branches were strewn across the road, forcing them to watch each step they made for fear of tripping. The path continued to show signs of neglect, until it disappeared altogether. All that lay ahead was obscured by trees. From now on, they would have to travel without a road to guide them.

As they approached the forest, Taren asked, "Will we be able to keep our bearings in there? It looks dense. We might not be able to see the sun at all times."

Zamna looked puzzled. "Is that the only way you navigate? By the rising and setting of the sun?" He shook his head, hissing softly. "There are many ways to tell which direction you're headed. We're going south, and the majority of branches on these trees are pointing in that direction. Lichens prefer to face north, but thicker vegetation will be on south-facing slopes.

We can also determine direction by shadows, and if it's night, we follow the stars."

"As long as *you* know where you're going," Taren replied with a shrug.

"You might take the time to learn in case I'm eaten by a bear," Zamna said with a hiss.

Taren's eyes went wide as he sucked in a breath. "There are bears in these woods?" He had never encountered one, and he had no desire to do so.

"I'm not sure," Zamna said dismissively. "I've never actually traveled this far."

Taren admired his honesty but wished the La'kertan had lied instead. It would be more comforting to think his companion was familiar with these woods.

Stepping inside the trees, he looked around, half-expecting to see the stone beast. This seemed like a perfect environment for him. Taren put the thought away. This forest was far different from The Barrens. Many wild plants grew here, and the trees were tall but less than half the height of the massive trees growing near his master's home. Here the land was wild and untamed. Vines grew long, wrapping themselves around tree trunks as they ascended toward the sky. Wide ferns littered the ground, pushing their way between massive root systems. The air was still, due to densely packed trees blocking out the vast majority of the wind.

Moving through the thick brush, Taren's eyes fell on many different species of plants that he recognized. When he caught sight of ripe blackcurrant, he had to alter course to gather some of its berries.

"Where are you going?" Zamna asked as Taren darted off to the left.

"Blackcurrant," he replied, as if his companion should already know. Quickly, he plucked at the plump, dark berries. He placed one in his mouth and sucked on it for a moment before chewing. "Mmm," he said, extending a handful to Zamna.

"We should be moving on," Zamna said, not taking the berries.

Taren shrugged. "Suit yourself." Opening his pack, he added them to the paper envelope that still contained plenty of dried fruit. "I'll pick enough for both of us, just in case." He continued to pluck berries from the bush. "You know these roots make good medicine. Mostly for female ailments though."

Zamna stood with his hands on his hips, waiting for Taren to finish collecting the fruit. "Hurry up," he said. Though he knew they needed to collect edibles along the way, he didn't want to remain too long in the same place. This forest made him uneasy, but he could not explain why. Perhaps it was simply that he hadn't been here before, and he wasn't sure what creatures they might encounter. He found himself glancing in all directions as he walked, trying to observe every bit of his surroundings. With a little luck, nothing would take him by surprise.

"All done," Taren said, rubbing his hands together. The bush had been picked clean, and his lips were stained with purple juice.

Rolling his eyes, Zamna gestured for the mage to follow him. They continued slowly, avoiding the thick underbrush. Taren occasionally wandered off to inspect the local flora. Some of them he did not recognize, and he wished he had his books with him so he could determine exactly what they were. Some of these might be hard-to-find medicines, and he may never pass this way again after returning to Ky'sall.

Finally, night fell over the forest, but the moon shone so brightly in the sky that they decided to walk a little farther before calling it a night. Zamna hoped the forest wouldn't prove too expansive, but after three hours of walking in the evening, he resigned himself to spending the night within the woods. Perhaps tomorrow they would find their way out.

"We might as well turn in," Zamna said, throwing down his pack near a tree.

"Should we build a fire?" Taren asked, already gathering fallen timber.

Zamna nodded and crossed his arms. He stretched his back and stared up at the stars. They twinkled silver against a deep-blue background, lending their light to the ground below. A howl broke through the air, jolting him back to reality.

"Wolves?" Taren asked.

"Probably," Zamna replied. "I guess we should take turns sleeping. The fire won't keep them away, and I'd hate to be eaten in my sleep."

Taren nodded. "I'll take the first watch. I'm not tired at all."

"That's because you're full of sugar," Zamna replied, lying down on his bed. Without another word, he rolled over and fell asleep.

Taren peered into the dark woods, wondering what other creatures might come awake at night. So far, they had seen only a few squirrels, and the birds had made their presence known through song. Briefly, Taren wondered if any elves might live nearby, but he knew it was not the case. The elves who once inhabited this land had left ages ago.

Nearly four hours passed while Taren sat in the darkness. When he felt he could no longer keep his eyes opened, he knelt next to Zamna to wake him. The moment he placed a hand on the assassin's shoulder, he regretted it. Zamna sat upright, his dagger finding its way into his hand. Before Taren knew what was happening, the La'kertan was on his feet prepared for a fight.

"Oh, it's you," he said, putting his dagger away. "Next time, don't touch me. Just make a noise or say my name." He slipped the dagger back into its sheath.

Taren nodded, his mouth hanging open. Curling up on his bed, he forced himself to close his eyes. Zamna could have killed him, or at least done him serious harm. He made a mental note never to touch a sleeping assassin again. In that line of work, he supposed it would be a reflex. Surely a killer would have to deal with people seeking revenge, and what better time to do it than when the assassin was sleeping.

After the fright Taren just had, he didn't feel much like sleeping, but he knew he had to try. Tomorrow would bring another long day of walking through dense forest, and he needed to get some rest. He sat up briefly to retrieve a potion from his pack. Selecting a vial full of deep-amber liquid, he took a small sip and replaced the stopper. That would be plenty for a few hours' sleep.

Zamna sat near the fire, his knees pulled close to his chest. He no longer heard the howling of wolves. Instead, a single owl hooted a warning to an intruder, and the crickets chirped so loudly, they were becoming obnoxious. Morning could not come soon enough for him. He was anxious to be clear of the forest, even knowing a desert awaited them.

This forest was not nearly as thick as the jungles on his island home of La'kerta, but it brought back more memories than he cared to have filling his thoughts. He found himself preoccupied, which could prove dangerous in unfamiliar surroundings. Once they were clear of the forest, his mind would be more at ease. At least then he could focus on the task ahead without his mind bringing up images of his past.

Taren awoke to the sound of Zamna calling his name. Though he hardly felt he had slept at all, the sun was shining, and it was time to resume his long march. Slowly rising to his feet, he pulled a strip of dried beef from his bag and chewed it. He offered one to Zamna who reluctantly took it and placed it in his mouth.

Chewing with a grimace, Zamna forced himself to swallow. Too bad he had eaten all the crickers two days ago. They provided more protein with a better flavor. Today he was determined to find some animal worth eating. If not, a squirrel would have to do.

Taren placed his bag over his shoulder and paused, staring at the trunk of a tree. The slightest movement of a leg revealed a fuzzy, gray-brown spider clinging to the bark. Its body was nearly as large as Taren's head, and its eight legs wrapped easily around the circumference of the tree. It held its position steady, aware it was being watched.

Noticing where his companion was looking, Zamna said, "It doesn't taste as good as it looks, I can promise you that." Taren paid him no heed, so he added, "It's venomous, and I'd recommend staying away from it." Seeing his companion still had not budged, he said, "It can jump three times its body length, and it will attack prey much larger than itself."

With a frown, Taren backed away slowly. The spider's many eyes glistened, and its pincers moved ever so slightly. Though he thought himself too large a meal to be in danger, he didn't want to antagonize the arachnid.

Taren came to Zamna's side with a grin. "It wouldn't really try to eat a human, would it?"

"Those spiders bite you once to paralyze you. Then, they wrap you in a nice little cocoon while you're still very much alive. After that, you slowly begin turning to liquid, until there's nothing left but ooze. The spider can slurp at that to its heart's content, even if it takes months." Zamna's eyes betrayed no lie.

Taren took one last look at the massive arachnid. Its venom might hold medicinal or magical properties. He would need only a few drops to test it. Getting ahold of the spider without getting bitten might be possible if he could hit it with his paralysis spell. Missing from this short distance would be almost impossible. He briefly considered running the idea by his companion but thought better of it. Maybe he would try it on the way back.

Zamna heard a faint sound in the distance and paused to sniff the air. "Did you hear that?" he asked, turning to Taren.

"Hear what?" the mage whispered. Both men stood perfectly still, listening to their surroundings.

"Nothing," Zamna said. Shaking away his uneasiness, he led his companion southward through the threes.

They walked on, stopping only once near midday to enjoy some nuts and fruit from their packs. Taren collected tubers each time they stopped, and he had gathered quite a store. They were not his favorite, but they were filling and nutritious.

Zamna took a liking to the new flavor. He crunched them by the handful and even started gathering them to fill his own pack.

As they resumed their course, Taren spotted a cluster of kudzu growing wild along the forest floor. Without a word to Zamna, who was walking a few steps ahead, Taren veered off to the left, making a beeline for the plants. He could already taste the tea he would brew from the lush green leaves. Stooping to pick up a handful, he hastily shoved it in his pack and continued to forage. There was far more here than he would need, but he wanted to get a good supply. His own plants had fallen prey to Master Imrit's goat, and he hadn't tasted kudzu tea in more than a year.

As he bent down to pluck a leaf, he was suddenly hoisted into the air. Crying out in surprise, he fell onto his back. Flailing his arms, he found himself trapped within a tightly woven net. Attempting to right himself, he managed only to turn himself sideways. There was no chance of finding his footing in the net. His legs dangled between the ropes, his hands clutching at the knots.

Zamna heard his companion's cry and stopped dead in his tracks. He growled low in his throat, angry that Taren had once again wandered away without saying anything. Dropping low to the ground, he crept in the direction of the scream, expecting to hear an animal nearby. To his surprise, he heard voices instead. Female voices speaking in hushed tones reached his ears as he continued to move through the foliage. Had these women harmed the mage? There had been only one cry. Perhaps the young man was too injured to utter a second one. Perhaps they had already killed him.

Rounding a wide cluster of trees, he moved with silent speed. Staying low, he peered into the distance. Ahead of him, he spied Taren dangling within a net that was affixed to a tree branch. He did not appear to be injured. Zamna shook his head, realizing that the foolish mage must have wandered into a trap while collecting some plant. Two tall women with broad shoulders stood near him, clutching spears in their hands. Zamna readied his daggers and kept quiet. If Taren managed to survive this, he would have to have a serious talk with him about watching where he was going.

Taren squirmed as the women approached, their weapons at the ready. He could tell by the surprised looks on their faces that they hadn't intended to catch a person. The trap must have been laid for some animal, but Taren had stepped inside it like a fool. With all his attention focused on the kudzu, he had failed to notice his surroundings. Now the question was, what would these women do with him?

They stepped closer to the net, allowing Taren a better view. They were large women, taller and more muscular than any he had ever seen. They were dressed in leather clothing with fur trim. Their faces were decorated with stripes and swirls of brownish paint, their short-cropped hair sticking out in all directions.

"Greetings," Taren called out, hoping not to make enemies. "I seem to have stumbled upon some trouble." He tried to hide the nervousness from his voice. Rather than assume these women meant to do him harm, he would act as if they were any other passersby.

The two women looked at each other and lowered their spears. "What are you doing here?" one of them asked. "No one travels through this forest but our own kind."

From his position, Zamna could hear every word. He hoped Taren would not reveal too much information to these strangers.

"I was just passing through," Taren replied. "Would you be so kind as to cut me loose?" The only spell he could think of to release himself from the ropes involved fire, and he had no desire to light the forest ablaze. Also, performing magic with these two as witnesses could be dangerous. He had no idea how they might react to a wizard. For now, at least, he would keep his profession a secret.

"Do you have a weapon?" the woman asked.

"No," Taren responded truthfully. His magic didn't truly qualify as a weapon. He'd never been in a fight, and he'd already proved himself a subpar hunter.

The woman who had spoken looked to her companion for approval before drawing out a long, serrated knife. Zamna tensed as he saw the blade but remained hidden in the underbrush. Observing her movements, he could tell she meant Taren no harm. She reached high above him, cutting the rope which held the net to the branch. Taren plopped to the ground with a thud.

"Thanks," he said, rubbing a hand against his backside. Untangling himself from the ropes, he worked himself free while the women watched, their faces displaying curiosity. Climbing to his feet, he extended a hand toward them.

The two looked at each other once again and did not return the gesture. A handshake was not part of their vocabulary. "You come with us," the second woman said. "You can explain to the Matriarch why you're intruding in our land."

"Certainly," Taren replied, glancing over his shoulder. He saw no sign of Zamna, who was still crouched in the thick brush. The women waited for him to walk between them where they could keep him in their sights. With their spears at the ready, they led him eastward.

Zamna followed close behind, maintaining a silent distance from the women. As long as they were unaware of his presence, he would have the advantage should he need to rescue his companion.

Chapter 6

The village lay only a few miles away to the east.

The women moved with ease through the thick forest, their pace much faster than Taren could manage. He found himself constantly tripping over the many obstacles littering the forest floor. Several times, the women stopped and waited for him to regain his footing before proceeding.

Zamna moved in silence, easily able to match the speed of the women. He kept a low profile, intending to remain hidden until some necessity forced him to reveal himself.

As they reached a clearing, Taren could see the small village situated just ahead. It was completely surrounded by trees, shielding it from the prying eyes of any who might pass by. The women led him between two carved wooden poles featuring dozens of different faces, each painted with bright colors and wearing a grim expression. The bulging eyes and protruding teeth usually meant one thing: death.

The village was filled with small, round huts crafted from native wood. Each hut was covered by a thatched roof, and the doorways were concealed by animal skins. Taren observed the women as they stopped in their chores to turn and stare at him. No men could be seen among them, and Taren wondered if they'd seen a male before. He stood at least a head shorter than all of these women, which further added to the spectacle.

The women paused outside the largest hut in the village. It stood at the easternmost edge, and two more carved poles stood on either side of it. The door opening was traced with intricate swirling patterns painted in blue. Most of the symbols were unknown to him, but he could clearly make out the moon and stars among them. Likely a priestess lived inside.

One of the women placed a strong hand on Taren's shoulder to hold him in place, while the second went inside the hut. After a short wait, the flap opened, and the woman stepped back outside.

"The Matriarch will see you," she announced. Holding open the door flap, she waited for Taren and the other woman to step inside before entering herself.

A woman in a tall headdress fashioned out of twigs and leaves sat cross-legged before a central pyre. The smoke rose to a single round opening in the roof, leaving behind a soft woody scent. The dirt floors were covered with a variety of animal skins, creating a soft cushion underfoot. The walls were adorned with wreaths, crafted from materials similar to the Matriarch's headdress. Some of them featured colorful berries, and at least one contained an assortment of feathers. Ritual items, no doubt. Taren hoped he might be welcome in this village, where he might learn more about his destination. These women obviously lived in peace with their surroundings, and they might have knowledge they were willing to share.

From his position in the brush, Zamna could see his companion being led inside the hut. He would not be able to hear anything that occurred, and that unsettled him. Daring to move closer to the village, he crept through the clearing and leaned his ear against the back of the hut. The sound inside was muffled, but he could make out most of the words. Unfortunately, he doubted he could intervene quickly enough should the situation turn violent. He would have to make his way to the front of the hut to gain entry, and there was little chance of doing so unnoticed. If he'd wanted to free his companion, he should have done it while still in the woods. Taren's calm demeanor had convinced Zamna that he wasn't in immediate danger. After all, those women could have killed him while he was caught in their trap. Instead, they had freed him and allowed him to walk alongside them to their village.

The Matriarch reached both hands over the fire and gestured them in a circular motion. Sweeping her hands through the smoke, she lowered her head and drew the smoke over it. After repeating the process three times, she looked up and observed the young man standing before her. "You are a wizard," she said, sensing his magical abilities. "What are you called?"

"My name is Taren," he replied.

The Matriarch rose to her feet and approached him. "You may call me Ursla," she said. "We are the Sisters of Gy'dan. Tell me why you have come here."

Taren wasn't sure how much he should reveal, but if he wanted their help, it was probably best to be honest. "I was just passing through," he began. "I am journeying south on a mission for my master."

"You are a servant?" Ursla asked.

"Of sorts, I suppose. Student would be a better word for it."

Ursla pursed her lips tightly, dissatisfied with his explanation. "Where did you find this one?" she asked the women.

"He was caught in our net trap about four miles west," one of them said.

"I have searched his bags," the second woman said. "He has nothing except food and medicines."

"No weapons?" Ursla asked, tilting her head to the side.

The other women shook their heads, and Taren smiled. "I wouldn't be much good with it if you placed a weapon in my hands," he said. "I'm an herbalist." He saw no need to mention any of his other magical abilities. It was best to keep things simple.

"You perform magic on herbs?" Ursla asked.

"In a manner of speaking," he replied.

Ursla came closer and inspected him with her eyes. "He is skinny, small," she said. "The magic I sense in him is not a threat. This man may walk among our kind."

The two women bowed their heads, acknowledging the Matriarch's decision. They turned and exited the hut, leaving Taren alone with Ursla.

"Does that mean I'm welcome here?" he asked.

"We will do you no harm," she replied. "You may partake of our food and drink."

Taren took that as an invitation to make himself at home. "Since we are trusting each other, I should mention that I have a companion somewhere in the woods. I'm not sure where he's gone. I haven't seen him since I trapped myself in your net."

On hearing Taren's words, Zamna decided it would be all right to reveal himself. These women were not quick to condemn a person, and they had easily accepted Taren into their village. He hoped they would do the same for him. Taking in a deep breath, he rose from his crouched position and proceeded to the front of the Matriarch's hut. A red-haired woman spotted him and shouted to her sisters. A dozen of them quickly surrounded him, blocking his path of entry into the hut.

Hearing the commotion outside, the Matriarch gestured for Taren to follow. She stepped outside and smiled at the sight of Zamna. "Is this your missing companion?" she asked Taren.

"It is," he said, his voice concerned. "Will they harm him?"

"No," she replied with a laugh. "They find him beautiful."

Zamna stood perfectly still, not bothering to hide his discomfort as the women ran their hands along his scales. One of them twirled a finger around the spikes adorning the sides of his head. They talked among themselves in hushed tones, smiling and nodding their heads.

The Matriarch stepped forward, and the women backed away respectfully. "It is long since we have had a lizard man in our land," she explained. "Many generations have passed. You are a creature of legend from our tales."

Zamna seemed less than flattered. "I'm no legend," he stated. "I might be a rarity around here, but there are plenty of my kind to be found if you know where to look." Being singled out as some mythical creature did not appeal to him. Never before had he been fawned over by women. Usually, those who were not of his race looked at him with either curiosity or repulsion, not affection. These women were openly flirtatious, and it was overwhelming. He much preferred to keep his distance from them.

"You are a sly lizard man to sneak into our village unseen," Ursla said.

With a sigh, Zamna replied, "I am a La'kertan." He objected to the term "lizard man," as it lowered him to the same level as a subhuman beast. "My name is Zamna."

Ursla nodded approvingly. "Zamna and Taren will stay here and feast with us tonight," she announced.

The gathered women cheered. Taren was flattered by their response, taking it as a sign of friendship. He moved next to Zamna and smiled.

"You should do a better job of watching where you're going," Zamna snapped.

"If I hadn't stumbled into their net, we'd have missed all this," Taren said, indicating the village with his hand. "A tribe of women living within the forest who think you are some sort of god." Grinning, he patted Zamna on his back.

"They never said I was a god," he replied. "They only said my kind were mentioned in their tales."

"I wonder where the men are," Taren wondered aloud. "Surely they have males somewhere."

"Maybe they ate them," Zamna replied with a wicked smile.

The women busied themselves preparing the evening meal. A large stag was hoisted over a flame, and rounded cakes of dough were baked inside clay ovens. The smells filled the two men's nostrils, and their stomachs rumbled in response. In a land with few visitors, they felt as if they were guests of honor at a feast. A woman with red stripes painted on her face brought them each a horn full of mead. She dared to give Zamna a quick kiss on his cheek before returning to her work.

The sunset created a bright-orange hue that lit the sky ablaze. The scent of roasting meat had grown so strong that Taren wasn't sure how much longer he could wait to eat. Luckily he wouldn't have to wait much longer. The first star appeared in the sky, signaling the women that it was time to commence their evening meal. Along with their guests, they formed a circle around the bonfire at the center of the village. The priestess was given first choice of meat, and she invited her guests to join her.

Taren filled his wooden plate with strips of venison and a second with a pile of fresh greens. Zamna followed suit, also requesting a refill of mead. The women were happy to oblige and filled his empty drinking horn to the brim. They sat upon log benches, enjoying the bountiful meal before them as the stars continued to appear in the sky.

Ursla took a seat next to Taren, a bone covered with meat in her hand. "How do you find our hospitality?" she asked.

Taren's mouth was too full to respond, so he nodded his head instead. Ursla seemed pleased with his response and smiled before taking a few bites from her bone. There were many conversations taking place at once, and the mixing of voices filled the air. The noise died down as five women approached the fire and began to dance. They stomped their feet and waved their arms, telling a story that was unfamiliar to the travelers. The movements were graceful at times and harsh at others, conveying a range of emotions through dance. The low beating of a single drum kept time, and the audience remained quiet and still. When the dance concluded, the women stood in silence with their heads bowed for a brief moment. After a suitable pause, the crowd applauded and whistled.

Taren wondered if the women always danced alone. In his homeland, he had never seen such a dance. Men and women danced together at various functions, but he had never seen any dance that told a story. Turning to Ursla, he asked, "What story did they tell?"

"It's an ancient tale of wandering," she replied. "My people traveled far to find this land. Many souls were lost along the way, but we have prospered since coming here."

He could contain his curiosity no longer. "Where are the men of your tribe?"

"They live separately from us," she said. "It works better that way. No fighting over mates. We hold a special feast once a year to join with them. We trade, mate, and share information at that time."

"I don't see any children among you," he remarked.

"A child lives with his mother for two years before he is given to his father," she explained. "The father teaches the child strength and hunting. After that, our daughters are free to rejoin us here. Boys remain with their fathers."

The custom seemed strange to Taren, but it seemed to work well for these people. He had no right to judge. His own upbringing had been atypical by human standards, and he felt he'd turned out well.

"Now you can answer some questions for me," Ursla said. "Travelers rarely come into this land. Where is it you are going?"

Taren glanced at Zamna, who was still gnawing away at the meat. He seemed not to have heard the question. Hoping his companion had no objections, Taren decided to let the Matriarch know his true destination. "We are traveling south to the tomb of Ailwen," he stated.

Ursla stared at him in disbelief. At the mention of the ancient sorceress's name, many of the women ceased their conversations and stared at him. Zamna had heard as well, waiting anxiously for a reply from the Matriarch.

"Any information you could provide concerning the road ahead would be appreciated," Taren said, hoping to fill the awkward silence.

Ursla continued to stare. "That land is cursed," she finally said.

Zamna leaned in, whispering in the mage's ear. "Careful what you say to them. We don't know if they can be trusted."

"They've been kind and generous with us so far," Taren replied quietly. "I see no reason to keep secrets."

Zamna sat back and said nothing. He hoped Taren was not making a mistake by divulging this information to the Sisters.

"If any of you know how to get inside the tomb, I'm all ears," Taren said nervously. "Perhaps the information is hidden in one of your tales." He wasn't sure what else to say. The crowd was still staring at him, and he could feel the redness creeping into his face.

"That land is cursed," Ursla repeated. "We have tales of Ailwen the Ancient. She is a being of pure evil."

"She *was* a being of evil," Taren corrected. "She died centuries ago, so there's little chance I'll encounter her along the way."

"Her spirit remains," Ursla said. "You must not go to that place. It is only death you will find there."

Zamna grew weary of the heavy conversation. Tossing his wooden plate to the ground, he said, "It's riches I intend to find there. Death is an afterthought."

"Lizard man should not make fun," Ursla scolded. "There is great evil in that tomb. You must not go." Her warm brown eyes pleaded with Taren.

"I must go," he replied. "My master has given me a mission, and I must see it through."

"Then your master is a fool," she spat. "He should have sent himself if he desires death."

"He desires life!" Taren argued. "There is an item there that can grant him eternal life!" Realizing he had said too much, he clamped his mouth shut. He had not even shared that information with Zamna, and in a moment of anger he had let the closely guarded secret slip.

Ursla shook her head. "He has sent you to your death. There can be no escape once you enter the tomb."

Taren sighed. "So far, I don't even know how to get inside. I may never even make it to the door." That much was true. Would Zamna be angered that he hadn't shared everything with him? If he had to travel alone, he would probably end up wandering in circles until he succumbed to the elements. He glanced at his companion, who was listening with interest.

"A vast desert lies before you if you continue south," Ursla explained. "It is a place of madness. If you manage to survive it, you will still be killed when you reach the tomb. No one returns from that place." She hung her head, lamenting the loss of ancient people in tales handed down for generations. Most of the information was embellished, but those tales held a significance for her people. Seeing these men so determined to walk toward death saddened her.

Taren took a deep breath. Hoping to ease her mind, he said, "I am willing to give my life for my master. He is dear to me, and I would do this for him. There is nothing that would please me more. It is my duty to journey south." With confidence, he added, "I have already seen my share of death. I will return."

Ursla looked up at him, nodding once. "I understand," she said. "We have no stories that will help you gain entrance to the tomb. All we can do is provide you with water and food for your journey. Tomorrow, I will see that you are blessed by our gods."

"Thank you," Taren replied, grateful for her assistance. Though he had no use for the gods of his own land, he believed the gods of this land might prove more powerful. These women had made a home here in a forest unfit for habitation. Their gods must be doing something right.

The women dispersed, each moving to their own huts to rest for the night. Ursla invited Zamna and Taren to sleep in her hut, while she preferred to sleep outside under the stars. As they entered the hut and sat upon the soft animal skins, Taren knew he would have to explain his reasons for keeping the symbol's power a secret.

"I'm sorry I didn't tell you more about the item we're seeking," he began. "I thought if—"

"No need to explain," Zamna replied with a shrug. "I have my secrets, you have yours. All I ask is that you not withhold information that might get us killed." He spread himself out on the furs, placing his arms behind his head.

"It's not that I don't trust you," Taren said. "Well, I didn't at first, but I do now. You could have walked away when those women had me in their net. You didn't. You came looking for me, and I believe you would have killed them all to stop them from harming me. I've never had a truer friend."

Zamna rolled his eyes. He wasn't the sort to enjoy sentimental moments. "Look, you are my ticket to a vast treasure. Why would I let that go? Think nothing more of my actions than that." In his life, he had few people he would consider a friend. In fact, he had none since leaving his childhood home. Perhaps Taren was a friend. He seemed likable enough, and he had yet to try selling him to one of his many enemies. It was quite possible this mage would have tried to save him, had he been the one caught in a trap instead. *What good is friendship?* Zamna had made it this far without a friend, and he didn't need one now. The two men could be companions for this journey, but nothing more. Zamna enjoyed his solitary existence.

Taren found it hard to believe that he meant nothing more to Zamna than a ticket to riches. From now on, he would be completely honest and keep nothing to himself. His companion had earned his trust and proved himself an honorable man. Taren lay back on the soft furs, his feet keeping warm near the flames. "I'll ask Ursla to bless you as well," he said. "Good night." He drifted off to sleep feeling more secure than he had since leaving the safety of his master's cabin. Despite the warnings he had received, he felt confidence in his mission and his own abilities to succeed where none had before.

Chapter 7

A rough hand awakened Taren at sunrise. One of the Sisters had come to rouse him and bring him to the morning ceremony. With a yawn and a stretch, Taren sat up in time to see the woman exiting the hut. She left the flap open, allowing the soft-pink sunlight of dawn to filter inside. Looking over at Zamna, who was curled up next to the fire, Taren smiled. For a hard-nosed killer, he certainly slept peacefully.

"Zamna," he called, remembering his past mistake. Never again would he lay hands on his companion to wake him. When the La'kertan did not stir, Taren called his name louder. "Zamna, it's time to get up!"

Zamna opened a single yellow eye and squinted it at the mage. He mumbled something inaudible and wrapped himself tighter in his fur blanket.

Taren stood over him. "It's time for the ceremony," he said. "Get up. They're expecting us."

With a loud groan, Zamna began to move. Finally he rose to his feet, walking groggily toward the door. The Sisters were already assembled, forming a close circle around the Matriarch. She wore an elaborate feathered headdress, and her face was mostly obscured by smoke. A low chant could barely be heard coming from the circle. Taren and Zamna approached slowly, not intending to interrupt the ceremony, which had apparently begun without them.

Remaining on the sidelines, the men watched as the women began to move in a rhythmic pattern, linking their arms together. Their feet moved in unison, taking them in a clockwise direction. The chanting grew louder, and Ursla spun at the center. Raising her hands toward the rising sun, she cried out in a shrill, piercing voice. Taren and Zamna exchanged glances but remained silent. With a fluid move, Ursla placed herself flat on the ground, her arms still extending in the direction of the sun. The Sisters followed suit, prostrating themselves before the sunrise. They lay motionless for several moments, and Taren wondered if he should approach. As he was about to step forward, Zamna shot him a severe look and shook his head. Taren stayed put.

Eventually the women rose to their feet once more. Ursla stepped forward and motioned for the men to join them in the circle. Both Taren and Zamna came forward to stand before the Matriarch. Before speaking a word, she drew from the fire a bundle of dried herbs that had been bound with twine. The smoke increased tenfold, filling Taren's eyes. Doing his best to suppress a cough, he squinted his eyes and tried not to breathe too deeply.

Ursla waved the smudge stick around both of their bodies, making sure to cover every inch. She circled them three times before placing the bundle back in the fire. Zamna appeared unfazed by the smoke, standing perfectly still with his eyes closed. Taren noticed for the first time that his companion had small membranes covering his nostrils. He momentarily envied the adaptation of Zamna's race. As a human, he had no such defense against the heavy smoke. It tickled and burned inside his throat.

The Matriarch flapped her arms in a birdlike motion. The sun had risen higher in the sky, its rays now focused directly on the two men. Taren was forced to close his eyes, shielding himself from the intense light.

Ursla paused in her motion and raised her hands, holding them with her palms facing downward above each man's head. "May the gods look favorably upon you. May you journey in safety through these lands. May the world treat you kindly and the spirits of our ancestors guide you on your path."

The smoke dissipated, carried along on a gentle morning breeze, and Taren felt it was safe to open his eyes. He beheld Ursla's shining face, her deep-brown eyes staring into his. Zamna appeared unaffected by the ceremony, but Taren felt a sense of peace. There was no apprehension about the road ahead. He felt only this moment and this place, where the Sisters of Gy'dan lived in harmony with nature.

Ursla reached into the ashes of the fire and spread them across Taren's forehead in a horizontal line. He had not noticed the pot of liquid that was steaming nearby, several yellow-green leaves jutting out from the pot. Bending down, Ursla retrieved a large leaf and offered it to Taren.

"Chew this," she instructed him. "Then you may enter the crystal cave."

Taren placed the warm leaf in his mouth, and an explosion of sour flavor nearly made him gag. Squeezing his eyes tightly shut, he continued chewing until nothing remained of the leaf. When he opened his eyes, the world was spinning. He saw double and then triple of the woman standing before him. Closing his eyes again, he hoped to avoid falling over from dizziness.

Ursla took his arm and led him away from the fire. The Sisters chanted once again, their song fading away as he moved toward the tree line. Zamna followed at a distance, curious to see where the Matriarch was taking his companion. He was well aware of the hallucinogenic effects of some plants; he had participated in a vision quest in his youth. He chuckled slightly with a hiss, knowing that Taren would not enjoy the spaced-out sensation he was experiencing.

Ursla continued to lead him eastward, where a large rock formation stood in the distance. There was an opening barely large enough for him to enter while standing. He stumbled inside, the effects of the leaves making his movements difficult. With each step, he felt he would fall on his face. Inside the cave was a single narrow path with little light filtering its way through. Blindly, he continued away from the opening

111

until sparkling crystals came into view. He had never seen anything like it, and though his mind was still reeling from the intoxicating effects of the herbs, he stood amazed at what he was seeing.

Shining crystals jutted from the floor and walls, pointing in several different directions. Some of them grew larger than himself. Running a hand along the smooth surface of a crystal, he made note of the coldness trapped within it. He was too far from the entrance for sunlight to enter, but the crystals produced a soft-white glow of their own. Sober, he would have been amazed by this sight. In his current state, he was astounded. Was this place real, or was it some elaborate invention of his mind?

Taren stumbled forward, making his way to the largest cluster of crystals at the center of the room. Leaning forward, he peered into the center of the formation, expecting to see his own reflection. Instead, an intricate, woven pattern appeared before him. The lines weaved themselves through one another, forming themselves into a tight knot. *The symbol!* Before him was an image of the item he was seeking. Though the crystals could not speak, he knew in his heart this must be what he was seeing. Looking up from the crystal, he saw the same pattern reflected in each crystal of the cave. A feeling of elation came over him as he peered back into the central formation.

Slowly, the image of the symbol faded, and darkness descended upon the room. The crystals ceased to glow, but still he stared deep into the darkness. Soon, a second image began to take shape amid the darkness. Soft lights swirled, forming the image of the face of death. Its rotting skin clung to the bleached-white bone of its skull, its mouth hanging open in an eternal, agonizing scream. The image shocked Taren back to reality, his heart pounding in his chest.

Pulling himself away from the formation, Taren ran through the darkness, his hand raised in front of him to avoid any obstacles in his path. Winding his way through the narrow path, he slowed just enough to avoid losing his footing. The light from the entrance finally came into view, and he breathed a sigh of relief. Glancing back into the cave to make sure the image had not pursued, he felt a chill race down his spine. Emerging into the daylight, he stared at the face of Ursla, who was standing outside the entrance.

Zamna stood silent, waiting for his companion to reveal what he had seen. From the look on his face,

Zamna knew it would be an interesting story. Taren appeared frightened and exhausted at the same time.

"What did you see?" Ursla asked, placing her hands on the mage's shoulders. "The cave offers many visions. I can tell you what it means."

Shaking his head, Taren replied, "Death. I saw death."

"No one can see death," Ursla explained. "It comes to you when it comes. You feel its presence, but you do not see it."

Zamna stepped forward and helped his troubled companion to sit upon a low rock formation. He felt concern for Taren's rattled state. Perhaps the drugs had been too much for him. The Sisters were much larger than the young mage, and they might have overestimated the dosage. "Is there medicine in your bag that will clear your mind?" he asked.

Taren thought for a moment and nodded. "A blue tincture," he replied.

Zamna hurried back toward the village to retrieve Taren's bag. Zamna did not believe Taren had blinked once since exiting the cave. Without a word to the Sisters, who were still gathered at the center of the village, Zamna rushed inside the Matriarch's hut. There, near the wall, was Taren's pack. Not wanting to return with the wrong vial, he grabbed the entire bag and raced back to the cave entrance. Opening the bag, he presented it to his companion. Taren seemed not to notice, so Zamna searched inside for blue potions. He found four of them.

Laying them out before the mage, he asked, "Which one?"

Taren did not reply, his eyes still staring off in the distance. Zamna reached up and grabbed Taren's chin. Pulling the mage's face close to his own, he repeated his question. "Which one?"

Taren appeared to hear him this time, and his eyes moved to the potions laying on the ground. He chose the one farthest right, pointing to it with his index finger. Without hesitating, Zamna snatched the bottle, pulled out the cork, and dumped the mixture into the mage's open mouth.

Taren swallowed and coughed a few times before wiping his mouth with his sleeve. "Awful!" he spat.

Zamna sighed with relief. Seeing the young man in a nearly catatonic state had troubled him more than he expected it to.

Ursla stood patiently, leaning against a tree. "He was in no danger," she declared. "But you are a good friend to him, pretty lizard man."

Zamna shrugged and stepped away. "Are you going to tell us what you saw?" he asked. "You said you saw death. Whose death?"

Taren shook his head. "No," he began. "I did not see death. I saw a skull. Its skin was rotting, and its eyes were hollow. It wanted me. For what purpose I cannot say."

"This is a powerful vision!" Ursla said, coming to her knees in front of Taren. "Bones are an omen of good fortune. Your journey has been blessed by the gods!" She grabbed his hands in her own and kissed them. Rising back to her feet, she said, "Come. We must tell my sisters."

They made their way slowly along the partially worn path leading back to the village. The women had watched with interest while Zamna rushed into the hut and left again with Taren's bag, and now they watched excitedly as the trio returned. Ursla waved her arms in the air in greeting to her sisters, and the majority of the village came forward to meet them.

Ursla proudly laid a hand on Taren's shoulder. "He has had a vision of bones," she announced. "He has been touched by our gods!"

The women cheered in response. They took turns coming up to place their hands on Taren's arms. The gesture was strange to him but not unwelcome. Their faces wore shining smiles as they wished him well on his journey.

Most of them turned to touch Zamna as well, and he did not pull away. He seemed content to stand, his lips pressed together to hold back his protests. Though he would prefer them to leave him in peace, he did not wish to insult them. They had treated him well, and he appreciated their hospitality.

Ursla led the pair back to the center of the village and implored them to sit a moment. "We should talk before you leave," she said. "The desert will be cruel, but our gods will protect you."

Zamna kept his mouth closed, but inside he did not believe in her gods' ability to keep them safe. Her belief was merely a superstition. Only his wits and knowledge of survival would protect them in the desert, along with Taren's magic. Relying on some supernatural being to come to their aid would be foolish. He hoped Taren did not believe in such nonsense. Observing his companions features, he could not tell how he truly felt about these gods.

Taren was more open to accepting the Sisters' beliefs. Though he knew better than to depend on their gods, he didn't see what harm there was in accepting their blessing. "I am grateful to you and your gods," he replied. Though primitive, these women were worthy of his respect, as were their deities.

"It has been long since our people traveled into the desert," Ursla said. "We cannot tell you of the dangers that you might encounter, but we can give you clothing that will be more suited to the land. You need something that is light in color to reflect the heat of the sun. Also it needs to be lighter in weight than this robe you wear." She felt the thick green fabric of his sleeve between her thumb and forefinger. "This is no good," she said.

Taren's robe was far from the most expensive attire a mage could own, but it was suited to many different environments. Containing magical properties of its own, it was not a garment he would easily cast aside. Still, the clothing these women offered him would probably prove beneficial in a desert, so he was willing to make the change and carry his robe with him in his pack.

Two women approached carrying small bundles of white material. "We have altered these garments for you," one of them said, extending a bundle to Taren.

As he looked over the white robe, he realized it was made of a woven material unlike the animal skin clothing the women wore. This must have cost them a good amount in trade to acquire. Gifting it to him was generous. "I thank you," he said.

They handed the second bundle to Zamna, who took it with a gracious nod. His scales would protect him from heat and sand, but he would not refuse their gift. Even an assassin knew when to avoid being rude. Besides, he might need to pass this way again someday, and he wouldn't want to offend the only people who could lead him through the dense forest.

Taren observed a hat in his bundle with a flap of cloth hanging loose. "A veil?" he asked out loud.

Ursla laughed. "That is to cover your face and shield it from wind and sand." Taking the hat from him, she positioned it on his head and showed him how to secure the flap.

Taren nodded, understanding the need for such a garment. Desert winds could produce sandstorms that would blind and choke him—a scenario he wasn't looking forward to. If he had Zamna's abilities to close off his nostrils, he might feel better prepared. "Thank you for these gifts," Taren said. "Your kindness is most appreciated."

"You will know you are free of the desert when a village appears to your south," Ursla said. "We traded there many generations ago." She shook her head, adding, "I would never believe a city dweller could make such a difficult journey through the desert, but the gods have given you a sign. I believe you will survive."

Taren felt slightly anxious, but he did not show it. He could not put too much faith in Ursla's gods, but if they were on his side, all the better.

"We should get going," Zamna said. "You've had your blessing, but you don't have this item you seek. So let's get to it."

"You're right," Taren agreed.

"At least stay and have breakfast with us," Ursla suggested. "There is much forest still ahead of you, and you will need your strength to get through the wild."

With all the talk of desert travel, Taren had forgotten he would still have to make it out of the forest. "We'd be delighted," he said, glancing at Zamna. "We have to eat," he added with a shrug.

Zamna replied, "Quickly." He was anxious to get moving and continue the journey. Taren would probably be content to stay here for weeks, and if he had to drag him away, then so be it. Relaxing in a forest village wasn't making the La'kertan any money, and he was ready to leave.

The women provided them with a breakfast of fruit and roasted meat. Zamna devoured his and stared at his companion as he took his time to taste each bite of food thoroughly before swallowing. When the mage had finished, he changed out of his green robe and into the desert attire the Sisters had provided. Instantly he felt cooler, and he thought the lightweight fabric might make forest travel easier as well. Laying his robe out flat in front of him, he retrieved a vial of clear liquid from his bag. While the Sisters watched, he placed a few drops on each sleeve and the tail while muttering a low incantation. The travel stains on the garment disappeared before their eyes. The women laughed and clapped their hands at this small display of magic.

Zamna scoffed, unimpressed by such a mundane use of a mage's abilities. "Will that same magic be able to stop a sandstorm once we reach the desert?" he asked.

Taren rolled his robe into a tight bundle and placed it inside his pack. "I doubt I have the power to control the wind," he admitted. "But I do know a few handy spells that I can cast should we need them." He smiled

121

up at Zamna as he slung his bag over his shoulder. "This journey is for me to prove myself a master wizard, remember? If the desert is as treacherous as they say, I'll have plenty of opportunities to prove my usefulness."

Chapter 8

Ursla provided Taren with a larger animal skin pack to wear on his back. Inside, she placed five bladders full of water, along with rations of meat, nuts, and berries. For Zamna she provided only two waterskins. Members of his race could easily go long periods without drinking. Though she did not know how long they would be in the desert, she expected Taren would have more need of the two skins than Zamna would. The assassin accepted them without a word, content to carry water for the man who was leading him to treasure.

"You can find more water for him?" Ursla asked the La'kertan.

Zamna nodded. "I've had some experience in deserts before."

Ursla turned to Taren. "If you get separated, look for birds. They will lead you to water. If no birds, look for other animals." Glancing at Zamna, she said, "Not reptiles. They don't go to water much. If you see hills, make your way to them. There might be a creek or lake at the base of those hills. If it's dry, dig down to see if the sand gets darker. If so, there is water. Keep digging."

Taren nodded, happily accepting her words of wisdom. "I have a few potions that will help with dehydration. I wouldn't worry too much."

Ursla's severe expression did not change. "Potions might work," she said with a shrug. "I've never used one. Remember what I told you, just in case."

"I will," he promised.

"Go and be well," she said, slapping him on his back.

The Sisters followed the travelers to the southern edge of the village, stopping as they got to the tree line. Taren turned and waved, but Zamna only nodded. As they stepped in between the dense trees, the women began to trill, lifting their voices in an unusual song. The sound drifted on the wind, fading away as the pair continued deeper into the woods.

Though the forest was as untamed as before, Taren felt it was somehow less wild. Knowing that the Sisters had made a home here changed the way he saw these woods. Though the undergrowth was as thick as ever, and he stumbled often on unseen obstacles, his spirits remained high.

Zamna stayed beside Taren at all times. It had been a matter of luck that they had encountered the Sisters. That trap could have been laid by less-friendly natives. These woods were expansive, and there was plenty of room for rival tribes to exist. The Sisters had mentioned that the men lived separately from them, but they did not say in which direction. Would the men prove as friendly as the women had? Zamna didn't care to find out. He would keep Taren close to avoid further trouble. If the mage attempted to stray, Zamna would stop him. Their goal for now was to reach the desert. Then they would worry about what might lie ahead.

For two more days, they trudged through the dense forest. Their travel was slow, thanks to the numerous obstacles in their path. The forest seemed to grow thicker before it began to thin. By the third day, the trees were becoming sparse, and the undergrowth had thinned considerably. They walked with ease beneath the shade of the trees, enjoying themselves for a change. Each step was no longer a struggle, and life was all around them. Squirrels scurried along the branches, and a spotted deer took a break from foraging to observe the odd pair.

"This is a forest I could get used to," Taren commented.

"Too bad we still have a long way to go," Zamna replied, continuing his southward march.

Taren felt rejuvenated as they camped for the night beneath the bright stars. The day's walk had almost been relaxing. There was no trudging on, climbing over fallen trees, or tripping on tightly woven brambles. Except for the day he had spent with the Sisters, this was the best day he'd had since leaving his master. He felt hopeful now. Hope that he might actually succeed in this quest, despite being the only apprentice to survive to this point.

Imrit had expected the trio to work together, but that didn't mean the mission couldn't be accomplished solo. Though, Taren wasn't exactly alone. Zamna had proved himself a loyal companion, and he was happy to have his friendship. From now on, he would consider this man a friend. After all, he had been willing to come to his aid when he thought his life was in danger. That had to count for something. He wondered what it would take for Zamna to consider him a friend. The La'kertan had seemed a bit more agreeable since leaving the Sisters' village. His manner was not as uptight, and Taren was sure he was coming around. Maybe soon he would be willing to share a bit of information about himself. Taren would like to know his companion better.

The night passed without incident, and a bright morning arrived to replace the darkness. Birds heralded the sun's arrival, and the air smelled crisp and clean. Taren looked around at the deep-green foliage. This was a place of beauty. Had he the choice, he would live in a land such as this. Imrit had the right idea living far from town. This place was an inspiration to magic.

"Time to go," Zamna said, snapping Taren out of his reverie.

Taren sighed. "I suppose so," he agreed reluctantly. Lifting his heavy pack, he hoisted it onto his back. As they pressed on through the forest, the trees thinned more and more until there were few to be seen. The sparse grass beneath their feet turned to sand, and they paused to take a last look back at the fine green land.

Before them lay a desert of red sand, stretching as far as the eye could see. The sky grew dark, and the wind cut through them as it ripped its way across the dunes.

"A sandstorm to welcome us?" Taren asked.

Zamna bowed his head and said, "It seems so. We should stay near the trees until it's over. I don't think we'll find much cover out there."

Taren agreed, and the pair paced back a few yards to take shelter behind a wide tree. Zamna retrieved the cloth hat the Sisters had given him and placed it on his head. This was no time to worry about fashion. The veiled hat would help keep the sand out of his eyes and allow him to keep watching the route ahead. His last trip through a desert was excruciating. He had learned to take advantage of any opportunity the barren land offered. This time, he was determined to travel more wisely.

The storm finally died out, allowing the pair to attempt entering the desert once again. Zamna bent down and removed his boots, revealing five long fingerlike toes. Taren couldn't help but stare at such strange feet.

"It beats getting sand in your boots," Zamna said with a shrug. He placed the soft leather boots inside his pack and stretched his toes, digging them into the sand. It was a pleasant, familiar sensation. In La'kerta, his people rarely wore shoes.

Taren briefly considered going barefoot as well, but the soft skin of his feet would probably be rubbed raw by the red sand. Before this journey, his life consisted of little walking and plenty of time sitting in a laboratory or library. He was by no means pampered, but his skin wasn't nearly as tough as that of his reptilian friend. Kneeling down, he placed a hand on the sand to check the heat. It was not terribly hot, but the sun was low in the sky. At midday, it might be scorching. Keeping his shoes on seemed like the best option.

They trudged forward into the sand, and Taren found it more difficult to maneuver through than the thick forest. With each step he sank, forcing him to lift his feet higher than normal to continue moving forward. The physical exertion was exhausting, and he doubted he would make it far at this pace. Zamna seemed to have no trouble. His feet were shaped nicely for navigating through sand.

After a few hours, Taren was begging to stop for a rest. "I need a few minutes," he said. "This sand is horrible." Not only had it climbed inside his boots, it had also made its way inside his clothes, scratching at his neck, chest, and thighs.

They paused to take in their surroundings. Zamna pointed to a spot a few yards to their left. "There's a boulder there that might block wind for a time. Maybe the sand isn't as thick over there." He didn't sound too hopeful about the latter.

As they reached the red boulder, Taren tossed his bag to the ground and plopped himself on the sand. It was just as deep here as anywhere else. With a sigh, he removed his boots and dumped the sand that had piled inside. His feet were raw with blisters that ached more when exposed to the air.

Zamna grimaced upon seeing his companion's feet. "Scales really are the way to go," he joked with a hiss.

Digging through his shoulder bag, Taren produced a small vial of orange liquid. Pulling out the stopper, he wrinkled his nose at the pungent odor of the liniment inside. Giving the bottom of the bottle a whack, he poured the thick liquid into his palm and rubbed his hands together. When applied to his feet, the potion removed all traces of redness from his skin. The relief was instant, the burning sensation being completely obliterated by the potion's healing effects.

"Not bad," Zamna commented. "Will it prevent future blisters?"

"It will provide something of a protective barrier," Taren replied. "But it can do only so much."

Zamna reached into his pack and pulled out the robe the Sisters had given him. "I don't plan to wear this," he said. "Maybe if you wrap your feet with it, they won't get so sore."

"That's an excellent idea," Taren said. "Thank you." He gladly took the robe and began tearing the bottom of it into small strips. Wrapping them around his feet, he tested to be sure his foot could still flex before shoving it back inside his boot.

Zamna stood to investigate the area behind the boulder. To his surprise, a few small cactuses were blooming with yellow flowers. Pulling out a dagger, he sliced off a segment and tasted it. The taste was palatable, so he cut off a few more and returned to his companion.

Taren took a piece and inspected it. "This is poisonous," he declared. "You can tell by the milky liquid inside it."

Zamna took another bite and chewed it. "Poisonous to humans maybe." He took the slice back from Taren. "It suits me just fine. You're welcome to my share of the rations."

Taren snacked on pieces of dried fruit and took a few sips of water. With luck, they would come by an oasis in a day or two. He had yet to experience the ravages of the desert sun, and he didn't wish to drink too much of his water in case it became scarce.

Storing the extra cactuses in his bag, Zamna asked, "Are we ready to move on."

"Might as well," Taren replied. For now, at least, his feet were in walking condition.

They trudged on for hours, not stopping again until well after nightfall. The coolness of the night air was a welcome relief, and Taren dreaded the thought of tomorrow's journey. They would be spending their first full day in the desert sand, and it might be difficult to find shelter from the blazing sun.

Before them in the distance lay the remnants of an abandoned city. Rows of square houses constructed of dried mud bricks rose high into the sky, some of them collapsing in on themselves. There was no sign of movement within, their inhabitants having long since vanished from this land.

"Looks like we've found a place for the night," Zamna said, leading the way into the ruined village.

The sand was not as deep as they reached what had been the center of the ancient town. At one time, this had been a hub of activity. Now, it lay dormant and uncared for in the middle of a wasteland.

"I wonder who lived here," Taren said. "Where did they go?"

"I don't know," Zamna replied, ducking his head into one of the houses. Glancing around, he added, "This one looks sturdy enough to sleep in."

"I suppose there's no need for a fire in this heat," Taren said, setting down his gear.

"It might keep the scorpions away," Zamna hissed with a grin.

Taren grimaced. He hadn't thought what sort of crawling things might live in this sand. Waking up to a scorpion on his face wasn't at the top of his to-do list.

"Don't worry," Zamna said. "I'll eat it if it comes near us."

Taren wasn't sure whether his friend was joking. The building they had chosen featured a small circular window facing out upon the desert. The stars twinkled above, providing a nice view of a desolate land. From this angle, it appeared almost serene. The light of the stars reflected off the sand, giving it an unearthly glow.

"If the sun proves too hot, we might want to move at night," Zamna said, unrolling his bed. "So long as the sky stays clear."

"That will help with the heat but not the sand," Taren said, removing his boots to find new blisters had formed on his feet. "I wonder if I should go barefoot too," he said. "The sand seems to be finding its way inside my shoes regardless."

"As long as you keep them wrapped to protect you from the heat, it might help," Zamna replied. "It might also allow sand into your wrappings, and then you're back where you started."

Taren groaned, not sure what was the best course of action. He rubbed at his calves, which were also aching from the day's exertion. In the thick sand, he had used muscles he didn't even know he had in order to keep his balance.

"Don't you have a spell for that?" Zamna asked. "You're supposed to be some sort of healer, aren't you?"

"In some situations I am," he replied. "In others, I'm just the person you buy your potions from."

"You do know a few useful spells, don't you?" Zamna was beginning to wonder what the point of his magic was if he only crafted potions.

"Of course I do," Taren replied defensively. "I just haven't had need of them yet." Though he had not mastered all the elements, he considered himself proficient with a variety of different spells. He could cast at least one spell from each school of magic, and he could cast several involving earth magic. His main focus had been on potions, but Master Imrit had made sure he learned a sufficient number of spells to protect himself. This journey was Imrit's idea, and he had trained his apprentices for whatever they might encounter along the way. Taren hoped it was enough. He didn't feel particularly powerful, and Tissa and Djo would have been much better with offensive magic. So far there had been no need for such spells, and Taren was grateful.

Zamna sat cross-legged, leaning his head against his hand. "A demonstration would be nice," he said.

Taren saw no harm in casting a small spell, but he couldn't decide which one to perform. There could be creatures around, and he didn't want to disturb them. Zamna's face grew bored, so Taren settled on casting a lightning spell. He focused his attention on a rock about ten feet away. Extending the fingers of his right hand, he drew energy from the sky. With a flash of silver in his eyes, he projected the magic forward, causing the rock to leap several feet into the air, bursting into dust. With a proud smile, he looked over at Zamna.

Zamna nodded. "Impressive," he said. "Let's hope you don't miss your target if we find ourselves in need of that spell."

Taren shrugged, remembering his failure to stun the spiny hog they had encountered earlier in their travels. He hadn't had adequate time to prepare, and the paralysis spell was more difficult to master than the lightning, at least for him. Next to earth magic, air magic seemed to come more easily to him. "So what about you?" Taren asked.

"What about me?" Zamna replied.

"You know quite a bit about me," he said. "But I know so little of you or your people. I hadn't even heard of La'kerta before I met you."

"Maybe you should look at a map once in a while," Zamna said.

"Tell me about your tail," Taren said boldly. Maybe if he asked a specific question, his friend would open up and talk.

"My tail?" Zamna asked, laughing. "You like it?" He stood and turned so Taren could have a better look.

"I'm sure it's quite nice," Taren replied. "Why is it so short? It looks like part of it is missing." At least the La'kertan was laughing. That should take some of the rudeness out of the question.

Zamna hissed with laughter and took a seat on his bedroll. "It's not much of a story, really," he began. "I wasn't much more than a hatchling when an eagle decided he wanted to see what I tasted like. He snatched me up, but his sharp talons cut straight through my tail, and I fell back to the soft nest I was born in. He got away with the end of my tail, but I avoided being eaten. Not a bad day, really."

Taren gaped open-mouthed at his companion. Was he serious? Not only had he offered up an explanation for his nub of a tail, he had also answered one of Taren's earlier questions. His species was in fact hatched from eggs. Assuming he was telling the truth, that is. "Are you making that up?" he asked. "I've never heard anything so outlandish!"

Zamna hissed with laughter, doubling over and holding his sides. "You humans have no idea about the people around you," he managed to say between laughs. Once he had composed himself, he held his hand over his heart. "I swear that every word I have spoken is true."

Taren shook his head in disbelief. "Incredible," he said. "That has to be the best story I've ever heard." With Zamna's pledge that the story was true, Taren no longer doubted him. What an amazing place La'kerta must be. Taren found himself eager to know more about the land and his unique companion. "Why did you leave La'kerta?" he wondered. "Is your family still there?"

The humor drained for Zamna's face, and he stared off into the distance. "We should probably get some rest," he said. With those words, he rolled over on his side, facing away from Taren.

With the lighthearted conversation at an end, Taren stretched himself out on his bed. Maybe Zamna would be willing to say more another day. For now, he would leave his friend in peace and not press him for information. The La'kertan was obviously a private man, and Taren didn't mean to pry. He wished he had brought along some books to keep him company when his companion didn't wish to talk. Instead, he resigned himself to the silence and looked out at the stars until his fatigue finally caught up with him.

Chapter 9

Morning in the Red Desert brought a vicious sandstorm tearing its way through the land. The pair could only stay low in their mud-brick shelter and wait it out. Nibbling at rations for breakfast, Taren stared out at the raging storm. There was no visibility beyond the opening to the hut. All was shrouded in darkness, the sound of the sand swirling and scraping against the walls filled the silence between the two companions.

Zamna ate more cactus, wondering how long the storm would last. He was anxious to get moving, though leaving this shelter behind was regrettable. They had no choice but to press on, but it was unlikely they would find such a perfect place to sleep in the days to come. Leaning back against the wall of the hut, he closed his eyes and let the sound of the wind lull him back to sleep. It was impossible to move forward, so they might as well rest.

The storm ended in late morning, allowing the pair to pack up and resume their march. Taren had drunk only one waterskin so far. Zamna had not had a sip of water since leaving the Sisters.

Taking a small sip of water, Taren asked, "Would you like some?"

Zamna shook his head. "When I get to that point, I'll let you know."

"I hope we find water soon," Taren said, putting the water away.

Zamna looked ahead and saw only a flat, barren wasteland. He doubted they would come across any water this day. He kept that thought to himself.

The heat that day proved brutal. It felt like the sun had reached out a hand to suffocate them as they forced themselves to continue on their way, trudging on for hours. Finally, drenched with sweat, Taren could go no farther.

"We have to stop," Taren said. "I need rest." His face was reddened, and his mouth was parched. Every muscle of his body ached.

Zamna helped his companion to a cluster of boulders, leading him to the side facing away from the afternoon sun. Reaching into the mage's bag, he retrieved the green robe that had been neatly folded inside. Shaking it loose, he laid it over the tops of the boulders, creating enough shade to help the mage cool down. "You must drink more," he said. "And take whichever potion helps with dehydration."

Taren nodded, pulling a half-full waterskin from his bag. Drinking every last drop, he set it aside and searched for the correct potion. Finding it, he took two sips before putting it away. "That should help," he said.

"You can't keep drinking so little," Zamna said. "It might be necessary to ration, but rationing to the point of passing out won't help. I can't carry you through the desert."

Taren scooted to one side, trying to make room for the La'kertan. "You should sit in the shade too," he said. The sun's heat was still intense, and his companion was exposed to its rays.

Zamna shook his head and squinted toward the sun. Before Taren's eyes, the La'kertan prostrated himself on the sand and vibrated. Fearing the La'kertan was having a seizure, Taren jumped to his feet. To his amazement, the reptilian man sank into the sand, burying himself to his eyes.

Seeing the shock displayed on his companion's face, Zamna raised his head and said, "The sand is much cooler only a few inches down." With those words, he lowered his head back down in the sand.

Taren sat back, shaking his head. An amazing race of people the La'kertans were. They were well adapted for many climates, much more so than humans. If he survived this journey, he hoped to one day visit the land of La'kerta and learn more about its inhabitants.

Retrieving another waterskin from his bag, he took a few sips to quench his ever-present thirst. The sun finally surrendered its place in the sky, allowing the cool night air to take over. The desert itself seemed to sigh with relief as the heat began to dissipate. Zamna finally came out of the ground, shaking himself to remove the tiny grains of sand that clung to his scales and clothing.

"I think it's best if we move only at night," he suggested. "We can move faster in the cool air."

"You think there will be more places to spend the day?" Taren asked. "I'm not sure I can bury myself in the sand like that."

"I'll bury you if I have to," the La'kertan replied with a laugh. "Let's get moving."

Taren put his robe away, grateful for the shade it had provided. He took a few more sips of water to keep himself hydrated enough to walk. For two more days, they continued this pattern: walking at night to avoid the heat, and staying low during the day, shaded by boulders or tall cactuses. Taren was quickly running out of water.

"You see that rock wall in the distance?" Zamna asked, pointing to the south west. "There could be water there. We should head that way."

Without argument, Taren followed his companion. He had only half a waterskin left, and there was plenty more desert ahead.

As they approached the wall, Zamna could see a dark streak running along the rocks. The sand beneath it was pooled with dark, damp sand. Smiling, he announced, "I think we've found water."

To their great relief, a small stream trickled between two segments of the massive red-rock wall. Removing his pack, Taren retrieved all of the empty waterskins and held them beneath the water. It took hours to fill them all, and dawn was upon them before he had finished.

"We'll have to stay here until sundown," Zamna said. "There's no sense in leaving the water behind.

Drink all you can, and make sure your skins are full when it's time to leave."

Taren couldn't be more grateful for this welcome relief. Though the water was not abundant here, there was enough to raise his spirits and give him the strength to continue. Pressing his face against the wet rock, he basked in its cool embrace. They would have to move to the dry side of the wall in the afternoon, but for now, he enjoyed the company of the water. Even Zamna took a moment to drink and splash water over his scales.

With the sun moving low in the sky, the duo once again took to their feet. They walked in silence until well past midnight, when Zamna suddenly reached out a hand and halted the mage from going any farther. Kneeling down, he gestured for his companion to do the same. Taren appeared confused, so Zamna had to point at the trouble ahead of them.

In the distance, a tall, lurking figure moved with a massive stride. It had long, apelike arms, its hulking frame covered in thick white fur. Taren could hardly believe his eyes. "A snow beast?" he whispered.

With a shrug, Zamna said, "I've never seen one before."

"I have," said Taren, "but I can't imagine what such a creature is doing here. They occasionally come down from the mountains when food becomes scarce in winter."

"We should lay low," Zamna suggested. "Maybe it won't see us."

Taren agreed, and the pair moved off to take cover near the rolling dunes. After waiting half an hour, Taren could no longer resist the urge to take a look at the creature's whereabouts. Unfortunately, it had moved closer. Ducking down behind the dune, he informed his companion. "I think it's heading this way," he said. "Do you think we can outrun it?"

"No," Zamna replied. "Its stride is twice ours. Unless it's injured, it will be on us within a few steps."

"Can you sneak up and kill it?" Taren had no desire to harm the creature unless it was necessary to preserve their own lives. However, missing the opportunity to be rid of it before it could turn on them would be unwise.

"It's harder to remain hidden from an animal than a man," Zamna explained. "Animals rely on many different senses, one of them being scent. With this warm air, it's going to be difficult to avoid detection."

"I'll have to use magic, then," Taren decided. "If it gets any closer, I'll do my best to subdue it." Peering over the dune, he kept a close eye on the creature, hoping it would turn away.

Zamna scanned the area for a better place to hide. He had yet to witness Taren's abilities in a fight, and he could not put his faith in the mage's skills. A few yards east stood another rock wall, though not as massive as the one they found earlier. It appeared to have a crevice at its center, and the pair might be able to squeeze inside. With any luck, the snow beast would not be able to fit. Tapping Taren on the shoulder, he whispered, "We should try to make it to that formation."

Taren nodded and stayed low. They ran as quickly as they could in their crouched position, making their way to the wall. The snow beast caught their scent on the night air and sniffed at the breeze with interest. A flash of white caught his eyes, and he observed it closely. To his delight, he beheld a man in a white robe, along with a second figure moving across the sand.

With a deafening cry, the beast pounded its chest before pursuing the travelers. The sound of the beast urged them on, and they ran with all speed toward the wall. Zamna squeezed inside the crevice easily, flattening himself between the massive rocks. Grabbing Taren's arm, he pulled the mage into the narrow opening just as the snow beast's massive paw came crashing down. His claws struck the wall causing it to rain sand and debris.

Angered that his prey was out of reach, the snow beast cried out again, his fury piercing through the night. Savagely, he clawed at each side of the crevice, peeling away the time-hardened layers. The pair had greatly underestimated the massive creature's strength.

"He's going to dig until he's collapsed the entire wall!" Taren called out. "We'll be crushed!"

Zamna looked deeper inside the crevice but saw only darkness. There was no escape out the back. The only way out was through the creature. Flattened against the wall, there was no chance of drawing his daggers. Not that it would matter much against a creature of such ferocity. His fighting experience was limited to humanoid creatures, and he had never hunted an animal without stealth on his side. "Do something!" he shouted at Taren. "You're a master wizard! Do something!"

The wall began to crack as more and more debris came crashing to the ground before them. With the wall becoming unstable, Taren knew it was time to act. If he did not, they would surely be killed. Though he had never had need to destroy a snow beast, he had learned that they were highly susceptible to fire magic. Mustering all his energy, he spoke the words to produce flames. Raising his hand to the level of his shoulder, he blasted a heated beam of red light at the beast. It roared in anger but was otherwise unharmed. Trying a second time, Taren closed his eyes to concentrate. A second beam, this time more intense, flew from his fingers, hitting the beast directly in its chest. It took a few steps back but quickly shook off the blow.

"It's not working!" Taren cried.

"Try something else!" Zamna called back.

The wall continued to crack, and debris was now falling from directly above them. Approaching with renewed vigor, the snow beast pounded its massive fists against the opening, shrieking with anger.

Taren searched his mind to come up with a better fire spell. He could find none. All that came to mind were frost spells, and the beast was sure to be immune. His magic reserves were running too low for a paralysis spell to be effective. Such spells required far too much energy for Taren to cast after such an expenditure. There was no time to drink a restorative potion, and his pack was wedged too tightly to fit his hand inside.

"Now, Taren!" Zamna cried, his voice carrying over the crashing sound of rocks.

Without hope of success, Taren mustered every ounce of magic within himself and focused his mind to the snow beast. Turning all of his will to frost, he shouted the words to the strongest spell he could cast. A beam of white energy erupted from his fingertips, blasting the massive beast away from the opening. It flew nearly twenty yards through the air before landing with a massive thud, spraying sand in all directions. Taren steeled himself for another attack, but the creature did not move.

From behind, Zamna nudged the mage forward. "Run!" he shouted.

Without hesitation, Taren forced himself forward and broke into a run. Behind them, the massive wall crumbled from the top, a huge section of rock tumbling to the earth. The crevice was completely blocked. Had they stayed in their hiding place, they would have been trapped.

Zamna leaned forward, his hands against his thighs, and coughed. Looking over at the snow beast, he asked, "What did you do to him?"

"Frost," Taren replied, still in shock that the spell had worked. Standing up straight, he felt lightheaded and drew in a deep breath. His magical stores were empty, as was his physical strength. Swinging his bag around, he reached in to find a restorative potion. Chugging down the entire vial, he wiped his mouth with his sleeve and dared to approach the unmoving form of the beast. Embedded in its chest was a row of small, silver spikes. Blood was still seeping from the wounds as well as the creature's mouth. Its eyes stared lifelessly at the stars.

Zamna came to his side to observe the beast. "Icicles?" he asked, touching one of the spikes. "It's cold."

Taren nodded, surprised by his own success. All of his offensive spells had been learned in books. He had cast only a few at targets, and none had proved so potent.

"Why didn't the fire subdue it?" Zamna wondered, remembering the sight of flames the mage had conjured.

"The land is cursed," Taren replied with a shrug. "My guess is the laws of magic have been altered somehow."

"What made you use frost?" Zamna asked. "I wouldn't expect cold to harm a creature from the Arctic."

"Honestly? It was all I could think of," Taren admitted. He thought back to his lessons with Master Imrit, and recalled a strange bit of advice the old wizard had given him. "Sometimes the least likely solution is the best one," he said. "My master told me that once, and it appears he was correct."

"Sounds like something a mad sorcerer would say," Zamna replied.

"Only someone who had tried and failed repeatedly would think of such a thing," Taren replied with a grin. He admired the tenacity of the old wizard who had experimented at length with so many different spells. It was that careful study that had led him to information about the symbol.

Zamna brushed at the dust covering his leather clothes. "What you did was pretty amazing," he admitted. "You saved us. No doubt of that." He turned to look again at the collapsed rock wall. Though it had taken some prodding, the mage had come through in a dire situation. Zamna felt a new level of respect for the young man. Previously, he had little confidence in the young man's abilities. His doubts were now gone.

"I did what I had to do," Taren said, hoping to glaze over his pride. He was impressed by his own abilities, but he didn't wish to appear overconfident or arrogant. Inside he was the same old Taren, a young man with an affinity for herbs and potions. He was no fighter, and he was not a master wizard yet. That title would come only after he had retrieved the symbol and placed it in his master's hands.

"You should probably rest after that," Zamna suggested. "You must be tired."

"Actually, I feel great," the mage replied. "That potion not only rejuvenates magic, but it also gives your entire body a boost. I could probably walk farther tonight than any other."

Zamna laughed softly. "Then you should probably make several more, and make a few for me as well."

Taren smiled and looked inside his bag. He had enough ingredients to craft only five more rejuvenation potions in addition to the ones he had prepared before leaving Imrit's cottage. He hoped that would be enough to get him to the tomb and back.

The ingredients were difficult to find and extremely costly if they had to be purchased.

They continued heading southward through the night and stopped to rest as the sun reached its peak at midday. The desert stretched on ahead of them, forcing them to continue their nightly march for a few more days. After what seemed an eternity in the wasteland, a village came into view on the horizon. They had survived the desert.

Chapter 10

Taren was overjoyed by the sight of the village in the distance. "We've made it!" he shouted, his voice elated. "A warm bed and food that isn't dried out," he added.

"It'll be a welcome change," Zamna replied.

The two moved quicker with the village in view. The deep, shifting sand gave way to hard-packed dirt. The town lay a couple of miles from the edge of the desert, but the walk was tolerable knowing there was an end in sight. Taren couldn't hold back a smile as sparse patches of green grass appeared scattered over the land. Though this area was not a lush green forest, it was the most beautiful sight he'd seen all week.

As they moved closer, they realized this was no village. What appeared small from their angle was actually a large city, spreading far to the south away from the desert. There was no wall surrounding it, which meant it was probably not susceptible to the sandstorms of the nearby desert. The city appeared to stretch on for miles, a welcome sight for Taren. Other mages might reside here who had knowledge of the tomb. Though he would have to use caution when inquiring about it; he knew nothing of these people except that they formerly traded with the Sisters of Gy'dan.

"I thought the Sisters said this was a village," Zamna commented as they approached.

"She said they hadn't been here in a while. It must have grown." Taren's feet met with the stone-paved roadways of the city. The structures before him were also built of stone, likely due to the absence of wood in this area. The buildings were sturdy as well as pleasing to look at. Taren felt at home among the cozy rows of houses.

Two towering stone posts bore a large sign engraved with the city's name: Yilde. As they proceeded farther inside the city, the buildings became more cramped. They were lined up neatly, but the sides were almost touching. Only a small animal could fit between the stone structures. People were scattered here and there, going about their various activities. No one paid any heed to the two travelers. Not even Zamna's strange appearance could draw their attention.

The people appeared human, but their skin was different than any Taren had seen. It was ashen-gray in color. He found it strange that they were not more bronze, considering the intensity of the sun at this location. He shrugged it off as just another race he had failed to learn about in his studies. With his head always buried in books about herbs, he had missed out on a lot of education. It was obvious the ancestry of these humans was far different from his own. With the lack of reaction from the citizens, he decided they must be well aware of the various races in the world of Nōl'Deron. Though it was not near any ocean port, Taren wondered if this city might serve as a center of commerce. If it had been worth the Sisters' time to cross the desert to trade here, the city must certainly have been special in some way.

As they passed by the buildings, a sign caught Taren's eye. A mortar and pestle painted in white upon a wooden sign signaled the presence of an apothecary. "Maybe the proprietor will allow me to use his equipment," Taren said. "I'd like to replace a few potions before we leave."

"Looks like there's a tavern ahead," Zamna said, pointing to a building a few doors away. It bore a large sign with a frothy mug painted in bright yellow.

"I'll meet you there," Taren said, heading up the steps to the apothecary.

A small bell rang, informing the shop owner that a customer had entered. Taren looked around and saw rows of shelves neatly lining the walls of the shop. Each shelf was filled with bottles and jugs of various sizes, and glass jars full of herbs and other items. In the farthest corner of the shop was a small laboratory featuring a metal table, mortar and pestle, an alembic, flasks, and vials. An open door into a back room revealed the location of the athanor, but Taren didn't plan to make potions complicated enough to require a furnace.

A skinny man with a long white beard appeared from the back room and stared at the young mage. "Yes?" he asked, his tone impatient.

Taren couldn't help feeling that he had interrupted the man. "I'd like to make use of your laboratory, if you'll permit me," Taren said. "I've brought my own ingredients."

"If you won't be purchasing anything, it's hardly worth it to let you use my equipment," the man replied, looking the mage up and down. "Besides, how do I know you won't break something? Do you even know what you're doing when it comes to potion crafting?" He eyed Taren suspiciously.

Opening his shoulder bag, he held it up for the apothecary to inspect. "All of these were crafted by my hands," he announced. "I am an herbalist from Ky'sall."

The old man raised his eyebrows and said, "I haven't had a visitor from Ky'sall since…ever. You may use the laboratory for a fee of one silver coin." He stood with his arms crossed, awaiting Taren's payment.

"Of course," Taren replied, fishing in his bag for the money. A silver was a lot to him, but he doubted the opportunity to use quality equipment would come again on this journey. With a polite smile, he handed the man a silver coin.

"Help yourself," the man said. Walking behind the counter, he sat upon a wooden stool to observe the apprentice's actions.

The setup to the lab was similar to that of Master Imrit's, only smaller. He suspected this area was for crafting quick potions at a customer's request. The bulk were probably made in an unseen room that offered a more comfortable workspace. He sat down and pulled out an assortment of herbs and some powders he had refined prior to leaving Ky'sall. It took more than an hour, but he managed to finish three rejuvenation potions before his neck began to cramp from the uncomfortable workspace. Rubbing at the back of his neck, he decided this would have to suffice. He'd needed to use only one so far, and he hoped there wouldn't be much need to use the rest.

Standing and stretching his back, he thanked the apothecary, who had not taken his eyes off the mage since he entered the shop. Making his way down the wooden steps, he walked up the road to the tavern where he intended to meet Zamna. The La'kertan was seated at the bar, a mug held high in his hand. Loud music was playing, courtesy of a five-man band on the stage. The tavern was packed with people enjoying the evening entertainment.

Zamna lifted his mug to his companion as he entered the common room. Taren climbed onto the high stool next to the La'kertan and looked around the room. They were the only two people who appeared foreign to this land. Everyone else had the same ash-colored skin and black hair of the people they had already encountered. If this city saw its fair share of foreigners, it must be at a different time of year.

"The food here is good," Zamna remarked. "You should get something to eat." He banged a hand against the counter to summon the bartender. "Meat!" he called as the man looked his direction.

With a nod, the barman disappeared behind a door, reappearing moments later with a large bone covered with meat. Taren accepted it graciously, looking it over only after the bartender walked away.

"What sort of animal is this?" Taren asked after smelling the unusual meat. It did not remind him of anything he had eaten before.

"A tasty one," Zamna replied, barely listening. His attention was focused on the stage, where two ladies were now dancing.

Taren bit into the meat and found it to be rather sweet. Its wild taste was unfamiliar, but Zamna was correct in his description. It was savory and satisfying to the mage's palate. The barman returned with a mug of ale, which Taren gulped greedily. It had a rich flavor that the young man found appealing. Before he knew it, he had drunk three mugs full of the golden liquid.

Zamna nodded approvingly at the young mage's ability to drink. The music went late into the night, the guests chiming in with tunes of their own. Finally, the bartender called out that the tavern was closing for the night. The musicians packed up their instruments and headed for the door.

Taren and Zamna had neglected to secure a room for the night. When pulling himself to his feet, the room spun around, forcing Taren to sit down once again.

"We need a room for the night," Zamna said. "Two if you have them."

"We're full up," the barman replied. "You'll have to look elsewhere."

"Where else is there?" Zamna asked.

"You can try the inn two streets over," he replied.

With a nod, Zamna helped his companion from his stool, squeezing his arm tightly to steady him. The pair stumbled out of the tavern, both laughing at their predicament.

Taren proved a poor navigator when intoxicated. After crossing two streets, he insisted they had not gone far enough to begin their search for the inn. Zamna knew better and led the inebriated mage in the correct direction. The pair stepped inside, only to be told that the inn was closing.

"Do you have any rooms for the night?" Zamna asked.

"All full," the woman replied unsympathetically.

They stepped back out onto the street, and Taren rummaged in his bag for something to counteract the effects of the alcohol he had consumed. Though his vision was poor, and the world seemed blurry, he managed to find the one he was looking for. His head felt much clearer within seconds of downing the blue liquid.

On a board outside the door, a poster displayed the image of a man with deep-set eyes. It offered a large reward in exchange for the man's death. Retrieving the poster from the wall, Zamna studied the face of the wanted man. "This man was in the tavern," he said. "I could claim the reward."

"You'd have to kill him," Taren said, coming to his side. "Why would you want to do that? He's done you no wrong."

"Apparently he's done someone wrong," Zamna pointed out. "With this posted so prominently, it must be no crime in killing him."

"I want no part of this," Taren declared. It went against everything he had been taught to take a person's life unnecessarily. No matter this man's crime, he would have nothing to do with killing him. In his mind, there were better ways of punishing criminals.

"This is a massive reward," Zamna said, holding the poster out. "Fifty gold pieces!"

"Surely the tomb will have more treasure than that," Taren said, attempting to change the assassin's mind. Perhaps it was impossible to persuade a killer not to kill, but he had to try.

"The tomb may have been raided centuries ago," Zamna replied. "I might come away empty-handed. At least this way I'm assured some gold."

"It isn't safe," Taren said. "We know nothing of this land." The last thing he wanted was for Zamna to put himself in danger.

Zamna seemed unconvinced, so Taren tried again. "If this man was easy to catch, someone else would have done it by now. Like you said, that's a substantial reward."

Zamna hissed with laughter. "Maybe there's no one around here with the skills I possess." He stood confidently, convinced that he would easily be able to finish the job.

"Don't do this, Zamna," Taren said, failing to find better words.

Zamna shook his head. "Don't worry," he said. "I'm not asking you to help. I'll take care of this on my own, and we can meet up again in the morning."

Taren sighed, wishing he had better skills as a negotiator. "Why don't we wait until the return journey?" Taren asked. "There could be treasure enough to last you a lifetime in that tomb. If we find it empty, we can return here for you to claim the bounty." It was Taren's last attempt. He was fresh out of ideas to convince his companion not to act.

"By the time we get to the tomb and back, someone else will have done the job," Zamna replied. "I've made up my mind. Meet me at sunrise near the city's southern border. We will continue our journey together, and I will be fifty gold pieces heavier." He flashed his pointed teeth at his companion and disappeared into the night.

Taren waited a moment, hoping the La'kertan would change his mind and return. Finally accepting that Zamna was determined to carry on with his plans, he made his way down the road to look for another inn. There were few lights to illuminate the city at this hour. Most of the inhabitants had already bedded down for the night. There were too many roads and too many buildings and not enough people to ask for directions.

Taren followed the only light he could see in the distance. A single lantern swung slightly from a nail affixed to the side of a barn. A man sat inside, a bottle in his hand.

"Excuse me, sir." Taren said. "I'm looking for a place to spend the night."

"Inns are probably full," the man replied with a hiccup. "You can sleep right here on the hay for a copper."

Wonderful, Taren thought. But it was better than nothing, and at least there would be a roof over his head should it begin to rain. Flipping the coin to the man, he unrolled his bed and laid it on the soft hay, a good distance away from the large pile of manure stacked in the corner. Unfortunately, he could not escape the smell. It permeated his nose and pierced his sinuses, making it difficult to sleep. His mind wandered to thoughts of Zamna and whether he had made the right decision in allowing him to go off on his own. He could not be a party to murder, but

Zamna was a loyal friend. He regretted not standing at his side, but he wasn't sure he could live with himself if he took part in killing a man for money.

Clouds filled the night sky, blocking out any light from the moon and stars above. No sounds could be heard throughout the city, at least not from Taren's location. Somewhere in the night, a man was about to lose his life, and Taren had failed to stop it. Though he would not be physically present, he still felt a degree of guilt. How the La'kertan could kill without a thought and never look back was beyond him. Visions of a weeping family and fatherless children filled the mage's head and invaded his dreams. Restless, he finally reached into his bag to retrieve a sleeping draught. Zamna's choices were his own, and Taren decided he would not hold himself responsible. Taking two sips of the deep-amber tincture, he fell asleep within minutes, his dreams no longer haunting him.

Chapter 11

Silently in the darkness, Zamna crept along the roads, his feet making no sound against the stones. Approaching the tavern with caution, he observed his surroundings. Not a single person was visible in the streets, and the only sound to be heard was the yowling of a cat in the distance. Moving up to the tavern door, he unwrapped a small set of lock picks that had been stowed in a secret pocket of his leather shirt.

Sliding a thin metal pick into the lock, he tested the mechanism for its complexity. Grinning, he realized it was a simple lock with only two tumblers. The owner shouldn't have bothered placing a lock on the door at all. Within seconds, Zamna sprung the lock and stepped quietly inside.

All was dark except for the remnants of a dying fire in the hearth. Though he did not know which room his quarry had gone to, he distinctly remembered the man climbing the stairs as he and Taren were leaving the establishment. If he had to search each room, he would do it. There was always risk involved in a hired killing, but for fifty gold pieces, it was definitely worth it.

His graceful movements allowed him to creep silently up the stairs. The wood did not creak below the weight of his well-trained feet. For years he had practiced the skill of moving unseen through the darkness, and tonight he put those skills to good use. This job was no different from the dozens of others he had taken over the years.

At the top of the steps, he crouched low, focusing his ears on the silence inside the tavern. Pressing one ear against the first door, he listened for the sounds of sleep inside. Cautiously, he turned the handle, opening the door a sliver. With one yellow eye, he peered inside to see a couple asleep in their bed. The man he sought was accompanied by two males, not a female. This was not the right room.

He crept down the corridor, checking rooms on both sides, but still his target eluded him. Finally, when he came to the fifth door on the right, he heard an interesting sound. His lips curled slightly at the edges as he pressed his ear to the door. Inside was the sound of snoring, and it was coming directly from the other side of the door. Running a scaly hand silently down the wood, he paused when his hand neared the floor. The weight of the occupant inside could easily be felt pressing against the door. This was the room. No other patron of this establishment would have the need for a guard to sleep next to the door. The man knew there was a price on his head, so he had hired someone to bar the door while he slept.

With quick but silent feet, Zamna moved along the corridor and back down the stairs. Tiptoeing through the common room, he let himself out of the tavern and back onto the street. Finding the city still deserted, he moved casually around the side of the tavern. A row of wooden supports rose up the side of the building near a row of windows. With one last look at his surroundings, he grabbed onto the wood and began to climb. His yellowed claws dug into the wood, helping him to lift his weight into the air until he came to the second floor. Swinging his shortened tail, he leapt through the night air, his claws digging into the wooden frame around the fifth window.

Waiting to be sure no one had stirred, Zamna lifted the window up an inch. The only sounds inside were those of sleeping men. With the window open half way, the La'kertan flattened himself and crept inside. Three men lay sleeping, one in each cot, the third wrapped in a blanket and propped against the door. He observed the face of the man to his right, only to find he was not the man on the poster. The man on the left, however, matched the portrait perfectly.

Drawing a dagger from its sheath, he approached the sleeping man, intending to slit his throat. Unbeknownst to him, a series of magical runes had been etched into the floorboard just beside the bed. They had no color or special glow about them. Instead, they blended into the darkness, leaving the La'kertan unaware of their existence. When the claw of his right foot touched lightly on the runes, a flash of green light erupted from the floor. In an instant, he was trapped, unable to move a single muscle. His eyes stuck wide open, and he could only watch as the men awoke and scrambled to their feet.

"What's this?" one of them asked, poking a finger at Zamna's tail.

"A La'kertan," the wanted man replied with a grin. "It seems he came to claim the price on my head." He knelt down next to the still-paralyzed Zamna. "You should have stayed at home." Flashing his yellowed teeth, he grabbed one of the La'kertan's arms while his hired guard grabbed the other. Dragging him to his feet, they laughed at his inability to resist. The runes had done a fine job of capturing the hapless assassin.

Zamna did not know how long the spells effects would last. Unable to speak or move his eyes, he found himself entirely at the mercy of the three men. Was this the same spell Taren had attempted on the spiny hog? Who had cast it? Never before had he tried his skills against a wizard. He might have thought twice had he known one of the men was a mage. With no magic of his own, he did not know a way to protect himself from it, other than staying out of the line of fire.

One of the men lit a small lantern to light his path and opened the door leading into the hallway. He stepped out to make sure the coast was clear before motioning to the second man. He stepped out as well, while the third man placed a pillowcase over Zamna's head.

"Can't have you seeing where we're going," he said with a laugh.

They lifted him between themselves and slowly made their way down the stairs. Carrying his motionless form into the darkness, they exited the tavern and walked along the streets for some time. Zamna's sense of direction failed him, and he had no idea where they might be taking him. What good was he as a hostage? He expected them to kill him where he stood, not cart him away to another location.

The La'kertan landed hard as he was tossed into the back of a wagon. His head still covered, he could not determine what other cargo resided with him. He could feel burlap against his scales, but he could not move a finger to tell what might be inside the sack. The men did not speak for the remainder of the journey. Only the sounds of the horse's feet and the wheel's against the stone path found their way to his ears. Eventually the sound of stone gave way to the sound of dirt. That they were heading away from the city was all he could be certain of.

Zamna began to count, wondering how far away they might take him. If he had any hope of escape, he would need to find the city again once he was loose. When they finally came to a stop, Zamna guessed that they'd traveled for about an hour. In which direction they had gone, he had no way of knowing.

"He'll be comin' around soon," one of the men said. "Best tie him up."

A second man dragged Zamna to the edge of the wagon and secured his hands with rope. Leaving the hood in place, they led him down a system of winding paths. Zamna could feel the effects of the spell finally beginning to wane. He was able to wiggle his fingers and blink his eyes, which brought him a small amount of relief. Soon, he could move his head side to side, and the pressing sensation against his chest disappeared. Coughing a few times, he made sure his voice was intact.

"Quiet!" one of the men shouted, slapping him against the back of the head.

Zamna said nothing and continued to walk alongside the man. Without warning, he was turned around and shoved into a chair, the pillowcase lifted from his head. His eyes beheld the inside of a well-lit cave. Through years of human usage, the cave walls no longer had their wet, living surfaces. They were bone dry with rows of lamps affixed at long intervals. A good portion of the floor was covered with water, and rope bridges were suspended between sections of solid ground. Turning his head to each side, he saw stacks of crates and what appeared to be a few different campsites. This cave must be home to a considerable population of criminals.

"Tell us, reptile," one of the men began. "Who hired you to kill my friend?"

Zamna did not reply. A man with two bodyguards already knew that someone had offered a price on his head. What did he need with such information?

"Who was it?" the man screamed, bringing his face close to the La'kertan.

Still, Zamna said nothing. If they were going to kill him, they'd have done it already. It was obvious the man had displeased more than one person, causing them to seek his demise. How else could he not know who wanted him dead? In truth, Zamna had no idea who had offered the bounty. All he knew was what was written on the poster he found at the inn. Presumably, that was the place to claim the reward after the man was dead. Zamna was not the sort to ask questions. In his line of work, questions could be more dangerous than the actual killing. Instead, he accepted a job and collected his payment rarely knowing the details of the hit. He wasn't interested in the politics of the game. All that interested him was the money.

The man he had intended to kill stepped forward and grinned. With a stroke of his hand, he slapped

Zamna's face, eliciting a hiss in response. The man laughed. "You thought you'd get yourself some easy gold didn't you?" he asked, still laughing. "No assassin can best me." Turning to his guards, he said, "Take him to the pit with the other."

One guard stepped forward and pulled Zamna's daggers from their sheaths. Checking his shirt for more weapons, they discovered the lock picks hidden in a small pocket and tossed them in the pile with his daggers. They took his pack as well, tossing it to the side to be gone through later. Then, the two men grabbed him by each arm, forcing him to his feet once again. They led him deeper inside the cave to a poorly lit area where the floor was damp and slick. A metal cage surrounded a low impression in the cave floor, and a single figure stood inside.

"Stand to the back!" one of the guards yelled at the man inside. He obeyed, moving himself to the back of the cage. The guard placed a key in the sizable lock affixed by a chain to the cage door. Swinging the door open, he shoved Zamna inside before securing the lock. They walked away, their footsteps growing fainter in the distance.

Zamna observed the man who sat at the back of the cage. He was broad-shouldered and shirtless with the ash-gray skin of the locals. His feet were also bare, but he wore a pair of tattered black pants. His dark hair fell in tangles upon his shoulders.

"Sit," the man said, patting the ground next to him. "It's not like you have anywhere to go."

Zamna took a seat next to the man and asked, "Who are these men?"

"Drug runners," the man replied. "They'll be happy to have you. It's hard to keep workers around here."

"Workers?" Zamna wondered. Apparently these men had a job in mind for him.

"Mining," the man replied. "There's a rare mineral in these caves, but you have to search deep inside to find it. The walls can become unstable in a second and come crashing down. We lost five yesterday."

Zamna shook his head. He had no plans to work for these men. As soon as his bonds were untied, he would kill every man in his path. A fight to the death was better than life as a slave.

"Don't think you're going to fight your way out of here either," the man added.

"Why not?"

"One of those men is a mage," he explained. "He draws traps on the ground that are invisible."

Zamna nodded slowly, realizing that was what had happened to him. Those men had been sleeping when he entered, and none of them had sat up to cast a spell. He must have stepped on their trap, causing it to flash and wake everyone inside. A careless mistake may have cost him everything.

"The men usually surround themselves with those traps so you can't get to them," the man continued. "We killed a few of them, but they always manage to round us up and get us back in here."

"How long have you been here?" Zamna asked.

"At least five months now," he replied with a shrug.

"What brought you here?" Zamna wondered, fearing he already knew the truth.

"Same as you," the man said. "I wanted the bounty. Fifty gold would have changed my life."

Zamna stared off into the darkness. The bounty had been a scam all along. Knowing he was constantly protected by a mage, the man had placed a bounty on his own head, setting the price too high for an average criminal to resist. Their "interrogation" had just been for show. Zamna could not believe his stupidity in falling for such a ruse. Here he was trapped in a pit, thanks to his own greed.

His mind filled with regret as he sat in the darkness wishing he had followed Taren's advice. Ailwen's tomb probably held riches beyond his wildest dreams. Now he might never see it. Taren would expect to meet him in the morning, but how long would he wait? Zamna had no way of knowing when he would be presented with the chance to escape this place. There was no guarantee he would succeed either. With invisible traps hidden throughout the cave, he might kill the men only to kill himself on the way out.

Zamna sat back in the darkness searching his mind for a solution. His best bet was to play along at first, until he was familiar with his surroundings. Perhaps he could find a way of detecting the traps. Taren would surely be long gone before Zamna found the way out, but maybe he would make it to the tomb on his own. Once the door had been opened, it might still be possible for Zamna to get inside. He hated the thought of coming so far only to fail now. Closing his eyes, the sight of treasure piled high in the tomb invaded his mind. For a chance at fifty gold pieces he had thrown away the opportunity to find an immense fortune. He chided himself, wishing he had taken the sensible route for once.

For hours he sat in the darkness, listening for any sound that might help him plan an escape. Voices came and went, but he could not make out their words. No one came within sight of the prison. Propping himself against the cold metal bars, he extended his legs in front of him. Crossing his arms over his midsection, he closed his eyes and waited in silence. Bouts of fitful sleep came over him, as his mind refused to fully succumb to fatigue. He wondered where Taren might have found to rest and how long it would be before he made it to the tomb. Would the mage find a new companion? Would he succeed in finding the item his master so craved? With a sigh, Zamna realized he would probably never find out.

Chapter 12

Taren awoke to the sound of a horse's whinny.

Opening his eyes, he saw a hoof less than two inches from his face. The horse dipped its head down to give the mage a good sniff before losing interest and walking away. Rising from his bed, Taren quickly changed back into his clean mage's robe. The white clothing given to him by the Sisters now reeked of the stables. After adding a few drops of potion to clean it, he rolled it and stuffed it into his pack. Gathering his belongings, he headed out into the city.

He and Zamna had agreed to meet at the southern end, so Taren headed southward along the road, hoping to come across an eating establishment. This might be his last chance for a hot meal, and he intended to make the best of it. Unsure when Zamna would show himself, he decided to check the area outside town once before settling in for his meal.

It was a long walk to the other side of Yilde. The streets were crowded with citizens going about their morning routines. Taren avoided the area near the bakery due to the large crowd out front. The scent of freshly baked bread and pastries was tempting, and he found it hard to continue on his way. With any luck, he would find Zamna quickly and then sit down to a hot breakfast.

When he reached the southern end of the town, he wondered where Zamna might be. There was no sign of him in the distance, meaning he was not waiting outside the town. Taren paced along the row of buildings facing the southernmost edge. There was no sign of the La'kertan. The hour was still early, so Taren felt no urgency to find his companion. It was likely he was still sleeping after his activities in the night.

Taren decided there was time to return to the bakery. The smell of sweet breads had not left his nose, and he could bear the craving no longer. His mouth watering, he joined the crowd outside the bakery, anxiously awaiting his turn at the window. After several minutes, he found himself next in line. He purchased a large chunk of cinnamon raisin bread as well as a sweet roll glazed with sticky sugar. Heading back to the southern border, he munched greedily at the pastries.

An hour passed and then another, Taren all the while sitting and waiting. Zamna was still absent, and the mage was starting to worry. What if he had got himself into trouble while trying to collect that bounty? Perhaps he had been injured or jailed. Taren rose and began to pace. There was no trace of the La'kertan. After a third hour, Taren decided to look for him within the city.

Making his way back through the streets, Taren stopped a few people to inquire whether they had laid eyes on the reptilian man. Most of them looked at him as if he had gone mad, but others simply shook their heads. Taren stopped by the inn where Zamna had discovered the bounty poster. Stepping inside, he found the place nearly deserted. Only one woman stood within, busily wiping at the common room tables.

Noticing she had a guest, she said, "Are you looking to secure a room for later?"

"No," Taren replied. "I'm looking for someone, and I wonder if you've seen him. He's a La'kertan, a scaly blue-green fellow."

The woman smiled. "I haven't seen anyone like that," she replied.

"Thank you," Taren said, turning to leave. Next, he would try the tavern where Zamna had gone after they departed, though he doubted the La'kertan would stick around after killing a man.

Upon entering the tavern, he discovered several men enjoying their drinks. He strode to the bar to inquire whether the bartender had seen Zamna.

"I haven't seen him since last night," the man declared. "Didn't you leave together?"

"We did, but we parted again and planned to meet this morning."

The bartender shrugged. "Maybe he left without you."

Taren thanked the bartender for his unhelpful suggestion. It was highly unlikely that Zamna would change his mind about accompanying the mage to the tomb. It was more likely he had run into trouble somewhere. The problem was figuring out where he had gone.

As he stepped outside, he noticed a bounty poster tacked to the outside of the tavern. It bore the face of the same man Zamna had gone to kill. Taren was sure the poster had not been there the night before. Was it possible he failed? It appeared that the man still lived, and the bounty had not been claimed.

Hurrying farther down the street, Taren caught the eye of the apothecary, who was standing on his porch with a broom in his hands. Taren approached the man to inquire about his missing companion.

"Have you seen a La'kertan around?" he asked.

"Seen?" the man replied. "No." Scratching at his beard, he added, "But I have heard."

"What do you mean?" Taren asked anxiously.

"It seems there was some trouble in the night, and the man you seek was involved." He motioned for Taren to follow him as he turned to enter the shop. Slowly, he shuffled across the room to take his place on the stool behind the counter.

"You were saying?" Taren asked impatiently.

"What does this La'kertan mean to you?" he wondered aloud.

"He is my traveling companion and my friend," Taren responded. "I would like to know what's happened to him." Why was this old man stalling?

"You crafted three potions yesterday," the man said. "I will trade what I know for those potions."

Was this man serious? Apparently he had been watching more closely than Taren thought if he knew what kind of potions he had crafted. "Why don't you just craft your own potions? You have the skill." He hoped to convince the man to name another price. The potions were difficult to craft and expensive to purchase. He might need them down the road.

"Yours are a superior quality to my own," the man explained. "I saw what you created, and they are far beyond my own skills. If you want to find your friend, I suggest you give them to me." The old man grinned and crossed his arms.

Deciding that the potions were less important than the safety of a friend, Taren retrieved the three vials from his bag and placed them on the counter. "Talk," he demanded.

"It seems your friend ran afoul of a gang of criminals," the man said. "He fell for their bounty scheme and was likely taken to the caves as a laborer." Scooping up the vials, he placed them underneath the counter.

"Likely?" Taren did not like the uncertainty of the word.

"It happens all the time," the man said dismissively. "You'll find the caves to the southwest of the city about four or five miles from here. They're hard to miss."

"How many criminals will I find there? Where can I find men to come with me?" Raiding a criminal's hideout alone would be foolish. Taren was no fighter, but he had to do something.

The old man laughed. "You won't find anyone willing to go out there. One of those criminals is a mage, and the people here are frightened of him. Had you come three months ago, when the market was booming, you might have found some foreigners to go with you. No Yilde citizen will help you. They would be risking their own place in the community."

"You're telling me these criminals are in charge of the city?"

"Not officially," the man replied. "But they do hold a certain amount of sway."

Taren had heard enough. "Thanks," he said, turning to leave. Not only would he have to face down these bandits on his own, he would have to battle another mage. It was unlikely he would succeed, but he had to make an attempt. Zamna would do the same for him.

Taren hurried to the southwest, passing scores of citizens along the way. None of them looked up or wondered why he was in such a hurry. This day was like any other for them, but for Taren, the day had brought an immense challenge. Would he be able to face an unknown number of enemies and come away successful? Was the apothecary even trustworthy? There were many doubts in his mind as he continued along his way.

Eventually, a system of caves came into view. There were three separate openings, and he did not know which to choose. Taking up a position behind a small rock formation, he observed the caves closely. After a while, two men came outside from the entrance on the right. They fiddled with the storage crates stacked outside the central cave before returning inside. If that was where they were going, then Taren would follow. If he had to search all three caves, he would, assuming he lived long enough to do so.

With his heart pounding in his ears, Taren crept forward to the cave entrance. Pausing a moment to listen, he heard no voices inside. Hoping the men had moved deeper inside, he entered the cave. There were enough lamps around to let him see where he was going, but the abundant light would make him too easy to see. Deciding that darkness was his friend, he closed his eyes and tapped into his magical stores. Summoning a slight gust of wind, he blew out the row of candles on the left-hand wall. There was no reaction from the men, meaning they were far enough away not to notice what had happened. He hoped his luck would hold.

A system of ramps and wooden bridges wound throughout the cave. Not knowing where to go, Taren decided to follow the most brightly lit pathways, as they were likely the most commonly used. Realizing there could be traps around, Taren cast a second spell to reveal any magical runes that might be present. That was the simplest trap a mage could set, and Taren was quite familiar with them. Only a truly skilled mage could hide such a trap from another mage. Taren smiled as the spell revealed a simple rune trap in the distance. That meant the mage might not be above his own skill.

Taren knew the correct spell to disarm such a trap and prepared it in his mind. It was still yards away, and there were more lanterns he would have to extinguish along the way. As he crossed silently over a rope bridge, a row of black iron bars caught his eye. In an adjacent room there appeared to be a large cage. Could that be where they'd taken Zamna? Altering his course, he crept toward the cage. Two figures sat inside unmoving.

191

Taren cast a second wind spell to blow out the candles illuminating the area. There were only a few, but he could not risk the light. As he approached, he could see the bars were covering a pit, and one of the men had a spikey head. Taren was certain he had found Zamna. Hurrying to the cage, he whispered, "Zamna?"

Zamna shot to his feet and approached the dark figure that had come to the cage. "Taren?" he replied, making out the mage's shape in the darkness. "What are you doing here?"

"Rescuing you," he said with a grin.

The second man came forward to observe the exchange. "Who is that?" he asked.

"A friend of mine," Zamna replied. Turning back to Taren, he asked, "Can you open that lock? They took my tools from me."

"I can try," Taren replied. Moving off toward the door, he lifted the heavy lock in his hands. "I'll have to blast it," he said. "It's going to make a lot of noise."

"Wait," the gray-skinned man said. "Can you use this?" He produced a small tool from his back pocket. It had been shaved to a fine point.

Zamna took the tool and nodded. "You should have given me this sooner," he said.

"How was I supposed to know you could pick a lock?" the man replied.

Grabbing the lock in his hand, Zamna needed only a few seconds before the lock clicked open. Smiling, he handed the tool back to his cellmate.

The man stepped out first and looked around. Without another word, he ran toward the cave's exit, disappearing in the darkness.

Zamna stepped outside the cell. "Are you up for a fight?" he asked.

"We could just leave," Taren suggested. The look on the La'kertan's face spoke volumes. He wanted revenge against his captors. "Or I suppose we could bring justice to a group of criminals."

With a grin, Zamna crept forward in the darkness. "I'm not sure where they're holed up in here," he said. "We'll have to find them."

"I already did," Taren said. "They've laid a trap to protect themselves. I can see the runes. With only one trap, it must be positioned close to the men."

"Can you disarm it?" Zamna asked.

Taren nodded that he could. His heart was racing, but he was not frightened. He found this moment exhilarating, and he was ready to test his skills against his magical opponent. What better way to prepare himself for the tomb? It was likely he would have to fight his way in. This man was no match for Taren, even if he was just an herbalist. He was also a master wizard, or was soon to be one. With a lifetime of training behind him and his friend at his side, he welcomed this opportunity to use his skills.

Taren led the way along the winding path, extinguishing torches as he went. Finally, two men took notice of the darkness and rose from the small wooden table where they had been seated. A third man stayed behind.

"There are only three of them," Taren whispered. This might be easier than he thought.

The men turned their backs to Taren and Zamna who were waiting patiently in the darkness. With a nod, Zamna sprang forward, landing full force on one of the men. Taren threw an energy blast at the second, sending his limp body flying down one of the corridors. As Taren prepared for the third man to come forward, he glanced over at Zamna. In a single move, he snapped the criminal's neck, his body dropping lifelessly to the floor.

"You didn't say we were killing them," Taren said. The mage had merely rendered the other man unconscious.

"These men collect prisoners and use them for slave labor. Those slaves die in the mines. This is justice!"

As he finished his speech, the third man came forward and cast a rune trap on the ground. This was no mage, Taren realized. He had merely learned to set traps. Had he been able to cast a spell to attack them, he would have been wise to use it. Using the same energy attack he had used on the other man, Taren blasted the third criminal, knocking him into the water beneath them. It was not deep, and the man had landed face up, leaving little chance that he would drown. Taren knelt and waved his hand over the runes on the ground. They disappeared, clearing the path ahead of them.

Spotting his pack on a stack of crates, Zamna said, "Those are my things!" He ran forward to grab his bag, noticing some silver coins on the table as well. Slipping those into his pocket, he said, "I think I've earned these."

"Let's get out of here before more of them show up," Taren suggested.

"Just one more thing," Zamna said. "They're mining Boohria in here."

Taren was aware of the potent, hallucinogenic effects of the drug. It was also highly addictive. Finding a steady supply of Boohria would make a criminal very rich, but their customers would die quickly. The drug was toxic in large amounts, and the users required more and more to feel the same euphoric effects. The only way to stay in business was to ensure a steady supply of new customers. "Where is the stash?" Taren asked. The kindest thing he could do was destroy it.

"Follow me," Zamna said, heading down one of the darkened passages. Stacked neatly inside burlap sacks were large chunks of unrefined Boohria.

"This stuff burns hot," Taren said. "Get ready to run." Reaching into his magical stores, he focused his energy to fire. Extending his hands toward the sacks, he unleashed a beam of red magic. "Run!" he shouted.

The pair turned to flee as the room behind them erupted in red flames. The cave walls rang out with thunder as the pair continued to run with all speed. Stumbling through the darkness, they finally found their way to the exit. The sun had set while they were inside, and the sky was filled with a soft orange glow. Pausing to catch their breath, both men leaned heavily on their hands, watching smoke belch out of the cave.

"I didn't expect you to come for me," Zamna admitted. He laid a hand on his friend's shoulder and smiled. "Thank you, my friend."

Taren smiled back. That was the first time the La'kertan had referred to him as a friend. "You'd have done the same for me," he said. "Besides, I might need your help on the road ahead." The two men laughed and slapped each other on the back.

"Let's get out of here," Zamna suggested.

"Gladly," Taren replied.

Taking once again to their feet, they headed slightly east before turning south.

"How did you find me anyway?" Zamna finally asked.

"I had to trade some potions to the apothecary," Taren replied. "No one else knew where you had gone." Pausing, he added, "Either that or they weren't willing to tell me."

"I hope they weren't expensive potions," Zamna said. "I might not be worth it if they were."

Taren said nothing. In fact, they were the most expensive potions he carried. A rejuvenation potion was a limiting factor in the magic business. Their exorbitant cost was yet another deterrent from the poor becoming fully trained mages. The man who could craft such potions was destined to be rich, though that was not the reason Taren had chosen to pursue the profession. It had come naturally to him, more natural than any other school of magic. The potions could be replaced; his friend could not.

Chapter 13

Continuing their southward journey, the travelers decided it was best not to attempt returning to the city of Yilde. They were sure to be recognized as the men who had destroyed the drug supply, thanks to Taren's refusal to kill the brigands. They would live on and easily be able to recognize him as the mage who had attacked them. Zamna would no doubt be recognized as well, since he was the only La'kertan for a thousand miles. Though he regretted not being able to obtain supplies, Taren knew it was best to press on.

Before them stretched an open plain of grass with a few trees positioned here and there. The routes to the east seemed the most traveled, as they would eventually lead to the ocean where visitors from other lands could enter with their wares. To the south, the land appeared wild with no roads to follow or people to encounter.

Two nights passed before Zamna was ready to talk about what had happened in the caves. The pair paused to rest beneath a cloudy sky. Taren produced a magical fire built only with a few sticks and dried leaves. It was small but warm and provided much-needed light on this dark night.

"I don't remember if I thanked you for saving my life back there," Zamna said, breaking the silence. He sat with his arms on his knees and stared into the fire.

Taren, who had been chewing hungrily on a strip of dried beef, said, "You did thank me, and you're welcome." He grinned at his companion. "All in a day's work, I suppose."

Zamna smirked. "I never imagined you as the fighting type," he said. "You really thought enough of me to test yourself against an unknown number of opponents?"

"I had to at least try," Taren replied. "To tell the truth, I felt better when I found out that the one calling himself a mage could conjure only rune traps. If he'd been a master wizard, we could have been in real trouble."

Zamna nodded and continued to stare into the fire. Though he hadn't known the mage long, he had risked his life to save him. That was no small gesture in Zamna's eyes. "You are the truest friend I've ever had," Zamna declared. In his life, he could count on one hand the number of people he had considered friends. Of those, Taren was the only one who would have risked it all to save his life. The others would have walked away without a second thought. Taren was a different kind of person. He was a true friend, and a man who could be trusted completely.

Taren smiled and said, "I'm honored to be considered your friend. You came for me when the Sisters caught me in their trap, and the least I could do was return the favor. I knew this wouldn't be an easy road when I agreed to journey south for my master, but it's been a better road with you along."

Zamna rolled his eyes. "Let's not get too sentimental." Hissing with laughter, he lay back on his bedroll and turned his eyes to the sky.

By sunup they were ready to move along. Their pace was steady and quick on the firm ground of the grassy plain, but they were forced to walk at a slower pace. The ground underfoot became damp and then soggy, and the grass concentrated itself in random clumps between shallow pools of murky water.

"I think we're in a marshland," Taren said. "This wasn't on my map."

"The Sisters mentioned a curse on the land," Zamna reminded him. "Maybe it's changed since that map was drawn." He had heard about the swamp, and it wasn't an area he had looked forward to entering.

"I suppose so," Taren replied with disappointment. A desert had been bad enough, but at least his feet had been dry. With his boots already soaked, and no escape from the wetland in sight, he knew he was susceptible to developing a fungus. None of his potions could treat such a problem. All he could hope was that there would be plants along the way that would help.

Zamna removed his shoes and put them in his pack. "Your feet will be just as wet whether they're in those boots or not," he said. "You might as well take them off."

"I might also step on something sharp," Taren replied. "I think I'll wear them for now."

With a shrug, Zamna said, "Suit yourself." He continued through the marsh, slowing his own pace to match that of the mage.

After stumbling repeatedly and landing on his backside a few times, Taren finally decided to try taking his shoes off as well. They were soaked through and heavy, which made his feet even clumsier in this uneven landscape. When he stood, he found himself firmly planted on the ground, his toes sinking deep into the mud. Walking was easier without the weight of his soggy boots, and he moved a bit easier over the terrain.

Crossing the marsh remained slow but steady throughout the day. When they stopped for the night, there was no dry material to bolster a magical fire. Taren settled for tearing scraps from Zamna's desert robe and rolling it into a tight ball. He used more magic than usual to create a hotter fire. All he could think about was getting warm on this cold, wet night.

Sitting with his legs extended, Taren put his feet near the fire, hoping the smoke would help destroy any fungi he might have picked up. Reaching into his bag, he pulled out a potion that was intended for cleansing wounds. Since it contained thyme leaves, he hoped it would still have enough potency to work on fungus despite their altered state. Trying what he had on hand was much better than letting his toes rot off. Keeping them dry during their march would be impossible until they made it to the other side of the marsh.

The next day conditions became worse. There were fewer clumps of grass to stand on, and the murky puddles were now more than ankle deep. The smell of the swamp was growing stronger, and Taren felt nauseated from the fumes. Zamna didn't seem to mind at all. He went along as always, pausing occasionally to see if his friend had fallen into a puddle.

The farther they went, the more mosquitoes they encountered. Luckily, Zamna had a taste for them, and his long tongue flicked in and out quick enough to catch four or five of the insects at once. Normally, Taren would have been disgusted, but today he was grateful for the assistance. The only thing that could have been better was an army of La'kertans to eat every mosquito in the marsh. Taren found himself scratching and complaining as they moved along.

As evening fell, strange lights appeared over the marshland. The pair paused to observe them. They blazed yellow in color, their pulses flashing intensely before fading out. The lights moved eerily across the surface of the swamp, enticing the travelers to follow.

"Bog lights," Zamna said.

Taren searched his mind, realizing he had heard the term before. "We call them will-o'-the-wisps where I come from," he replied. "I've read about them, but I've never seen them."

"They can be troublesome," Zamna warned. "It's best to ignore them."

"I've read they can be helpful at times," Taren stated. "Some travelers report the lights leading them away from danger rather than into it."

Zamna looked at him in disbelief. "I've never heard anything good about them. They must be different in your land."

Taren shrugged. "It's probably best to avoid them," he agreed. These were magical beings of unknown purpose. It would be unwise to follow them expecting to be led out of the marsh.

The duo continued southward, doing their best to ignore the lights. As they continued through the swamp, the lights crept closer, eventually revealing themselves to the travelers. Tiny winged fairies with sinister grins buzzed around them, diving in close before zipping away. They had jagged, pointy teeth and thin wisps of brown hair drawn tightly on top of their heads. Their wings were luminescent, with yellow veins running through them.

They came so close to his face that Zamna had to resist the urge to taste one. Certainly they would be easy to catch, but he had never knowingly eaten a magical creature. The threatening expression each fairy wore on its face was enough to make him think twice. Though it would have been easy to swat them from the air, he chose to continue his attempt to ignore them and focus his eyes on the land ahead.

Neither man suggested stopping to rest for the night. Both were anxious to be out of the marsh, or at least away from the menacing fairies. They moved along without speaking, hoping each step would take them farther from the tiny pests, but still the devils pursued.

They sloshed along through the darkness with only the light of the fairies to illuminate their path. A wave of exhaustion crept over Taren, buckling his knees from beneath him. With a soft splash, he fell over on his side fast asleep. Zamna could only watch as his friend teetered over. His arms felt too heavy to reach out and help the mage. He soon followed suit, landing on his back on a patch of wet grass.

The magic of the fairies had forced the travelers into this unconscious state. While the two men lay motionless on the ground, the winged creatures

206

surrounded their forms, preparing to sink their teeth into their victims' hides. The La'kertan's scales proved too much of an obstacle for the impatient fairies, so they moved over to feast on the human instead. They found him much more palatable, thanks to the magical energy stored inside him. Greedily they drank from him until their bellies could hold no more. Most of them flew away, leaving a faint trail of yellow light behind them.

At dawn, Zamna came to with the sound of buzzing in his ears. A single fairy still buzzed over Taren's sleeping form. Though still groggy, Zamna extended a hand and swatted at the creature, forcing it away from his companion. It giggled softly before flying away and disappearing somewhere over the marsh.

Placing a hand on Taren's shoulder, Zamna shook him gently. "Wake up," he said. "We have to get out of here before they come back."

Taren awoke confused and disoriented. When he attempted to sit up, he found himself too drained to do so and flopped back onto the soggy ground.

"Easy," Zamna said, helping his friend sit up.

Taren sat wearily, his head drooping loosely over his chest. Through his woozy vision, he observed tiny bite marks on his hands. Pulling back his sleeves, he discovered that his arms were covered in hundreds of tiny bites.

Zamna took notice of the tooth marks as well. "They bit you?" he asked, confused. Looking at his own arms, he saw no such marks. His scales had apparently been too tough for the tiny monsters to penetrate.

"They drained my magic," Taren said, still in shock. "It's the only explanation."

"You'll have to take one of your potions, maybe two," Zamna said. "We need to get moving. I want out of this swamp before another night falls." The words were meaningless considering he had no idea how large the swamp actually was. Still, he was determined to get moving and find his way out as quickly as possible.

Taren hesitated when Zamna placed his pack before him. He feared wasting a rejuvenation potion that he might need later. What if they were put in a more desperate situation? Of course this situation was fairly desperate. He felt like he'd been run down by a herd of wild horses, and he doubted he would be moving from this spot soon. The fairies would undoubtedly return at dusk to sap the small amount of energy he had recovered.

Zamna opened the bag and pressed it against Taren's chest. "Drink," he said. "One of these has to fix this."

Reluctantly, Taren reached into the bag and retrieved a rejuvenation potion. Being too weak to down the whole thing at once, he slowly sipped at the contents. This one had a fruity taste that was not unpleasant at all. He smiled to himself, knowing how valuable this potion truly was. In minutes, he felt himself completely recovered. With renewed vigor, he uncorked a vial of green liquid and rubbed its contents over his skin. The tiny bite marks faded until they were nothing more than a memory.

"Feel better?" Zamna asked with concern.

Taren nodded. "I just hope I don't regret using that potion. I might need it later."

"You wouldn't be much good the way you were," Zamna replied. "At least now we can get moving."

Taren rose to his feet and situated his pack for the long march ahead. Zamna took a moment to get his bearings before leading his companion southward.

"If we aren't out of here by night, we might have to fight those things," Zamna stated. "I should have eaten them last night before they had the chance to feast on you."

Taren laughed. "I'm not sure they would have stayed down. Who knows what those things might do to your insides?"

Zamna wondered why they had acted the way they did. "Do those things normally drain magic?"

"I don't know, to be honest," Taren replied. "I've heard of them leading men to their deaths. Perhaps they suck out all of their energy and leave them to die. I was lucky to have potions with me."

"Would your magic recover without the potion?" Zamna asked.

"Eventually," Taren said. "It would take several days, though. Elves can recover spent magic much faster." Again he remembered his silly childhood dream of turning into an elf to improve his magical abilities. Unfortunately, it would have required at least a hundred years of intense study to achieve the rank of master had he been an elf. As a human, he would be lucky to live that long. An elf's training was far different from his own. He shook his head, wondering if he would ever forget such an idle dream.

"I don't plan to stick around for days if I can avoid it," Zamna declared. "It's best that you used that potion. If we do have to fight them tonight, you'll have your full strength."

To their relief, they encountered no more fairies as they passed through the swamp. It would be two more days before the land began to dry out and they found themselves on firm ground for a change. The grass here was thick and deep green, thanks to the minerals it collected from the nearby bog. The smell, however, did not leave their nostrils. The stench of rotting vegetation and whatever else might be hiding in the swamp still wafted through the air. The pair found themselves still anxious to put distance between themselves and the marsh.

Another day of travel brought them within sight of a lake. As they drew closer, Taren could see it was not filled with water. Instead, it held a putrid, yellow-green liquid that smelled worse than the bog ever had. Clamping his hand over his nose and mouth, he fought back the urge to retch.

Zamna was not immune to the stench. "What is this place?" he asked, fearing his companion would not have the answer. "Is this on your map?"

Taren pulled the map out of his bag. "It's called The Rotting Lake," he said. "I guess we know why." Putting the map away, he once again covered his nose and mouth with his hand to block out the disgusting smell. "The faster we can cross, the faster we can get away from the smell," Taren said through his fingers. The true question was, how would they get across the lake? There were no boats or docks nearby, which meant no one was crossing this lake on a regular basis. Assuming anyone lived in this area, it wasn't surprising they would stay far away from the lake.

"I could swim it," Zamna said. "I might wish I hadn't, but I could do it." Being born on an island, he had spent many hours swimming in the ocean in his youth. He knew himself to be a strong swimmer, but the liquid before him could be toxic. The thought of stepping into it nearly made him ill.

"I can't swim," Taren admitted. In all his years of schooling, he had never bothered to learn. If he had become a water mage, he might have found the skill useful. Instead he had focused on keeping his feet firmly planted on the earth. "We'll have to build a raft."

The two men looked around but found no materials that could be used for a raft. A few trees stood tall, but they had no way of cutting them down or removing their branches. Taren briefly considered using fire to topple one, but burnt limbs would serve poorly for a raft.

With a sigh, Zamna said, "I could swim to the far bank and see if there is anything there that could be used to get you across." He still dreaded the thought of entering the lake, but it seemed like that would be his only choice.

Taren stepped forward toward the lake. "Let me check the water first," he said. "I might be able to determine if it's toxic." He produced an empty vial from his bag and knelt down next to the yellow liquid. Reaching the vial forward, he touched the mouth of it to the water and drew out a small amount. When he lifted the vial away from the surface, the ground began to shake.

The pair crouched low to maintain their footing as the rumbling continued. As they watched in stunned silence, a giant stone-gray hand lifted itself from the center of the lake, its massive palm facing upward. Slowly, the hand made its way across the lake, approaching the bank where the travelers stood. It came to a halt in the shallows and lowered itself down to the surface of the water, its fingers reaching the land near Taren's feet. He stared at it a moment longer, amazed by what he had just witnessed. Staring at the upturned hand, he knew what he had to do.

Chapter 14

Cautiously Taren stepped forward, placing a foot on one of the outstretched stone fingers. Zamna extended an arm as if to stop him, but Taren shook his head.

"It's all right," Taren assured him. "It will take us to the other side." He climbed onto the fingers and moved to sit upon the palm.

Zamna eyed his friend suspiciously. "Are you sure it's safe?" he asked, approaching warily.

"Yes," Taren replied, motioning for him to come aboard.

Reluctantly, Zamna stepped up onto the fingers and made his way next to the mage. Slowly he took a seat. As soon as he was down, the hand began to move, lifting itself to a height several feet above the surface. In a smooth motion, it carried them out over the lake. Looking down, they observed the swirling yellow-green liquid below them. Small puffs of greenish smoke rose from the surface, dissipating a few inches above the fetid water. Surprisingly, the smell was less intense from above the lake's surface. The bog on the other side must have contributed to the majority of the stench.

The hand moved at a snail's pace, which made Zamna even more anxious. "I wish this thing would move faster," he commented.

"It probably just doesn't want to jostle us too much," Taren suggested. "Most people aren't accustomed to this form of travel, I'd assume."

"Well, I'll be happier to be back on land," the La'kertan said, staring at the far bank.

As they approached the far side, Taren beheld a wide green prairie stretching on before them. His heart lifted as he looked forward to setting foot on the promising land ahead. It was far more inviting than some of the other landscapes they'd encountered.

The stone hand finally came to a halt and lowered itself to a height even with the bank. The travelers hurried off their strange boat and turned to watch as it sank back into the depths.

"Thank you," Taren called after it, not knowing whether it had any type of consciousness. It was best to be polite, just in case. He might need a ride back to the other side someday.

As he moved away from the bank, Zamna straightened his pack. "How did you know that thing wouldn't crush us or drown us?"

"I didn't," Taren admitted.

Zamna shot him a sharp look. "You didn't know?"

"No," he replied with a grin. "It seemed the most logical course."

Zamna shook his head and pursed his lips, unsure how to respond. The mage had gambled both their lives, but he had turned out to be correct. He admired the young man's gumption. Persuading the La'kertan to follow had taken nearly no effort. He had simply trusted in the mage's decision—a decision that had brought them both safely across The Rotting Lake.

With their feet on solid ground, they continued their southward march. Taren stopped repeatedly to collect flowers and leaves that might prove useful for potions. Though he didn't expect to find the proper equipment, he preferred to travel prepared. Passing up these ingredients would be silly when they held medicinal properties despite not being processed.

The prairie grass reached up to their knees, and a gentle breeze caressed the stalks as they moved past. The weather was delightful, with a bright sun shining and puffy clouds drifting overhead. Butterflies in a variety of colors floated lazily on the breeze, stopping for an occasional sip from a fragrant bloom. Shades of pink, yellow, and blue were scattered throughout the green, plotting a course for the travelers as they walked in serene silence.

The land surpassed the forests in beauty, at least in Taren's mind. Here was a land of tranquility and open spaces, where a mage could find both solitude and comfort. For an herbalist, there were few landscapes more appealing than a meadow. Here the ingredients grew wild and strong without the need for human intervention. Once, he had read a text that suggested even the finest artificial gardens produced a weaker variety of herbs. It went on to explain how human intervention negated the need for the plant to survive on its own merits. In the wild, only the strongest, healthiest individuals would survive. This land was like a treasure trove to the young herbalist. A plethora of the finest ingredients Nōl'Deron had to offer lay before him, ripe for the taking. A more blissful land he had never seen.

For an entire day, they basked in the serenity of the prairie. By the second day, the land was dotted once again with farmhouses and green fields. There was likely a town nearby, but they knew neither in which direction it lay, nor how many days off-course it would take them.

"If we need supplies, you could approach one of the farms," Zamna suggested. "I should stay back, in case they aren't familiar with my kind."

"I've found so much in the meadow that I doubt there's anything I need," Taren replied. "All of these items are edible, and we still have nuts and fruit. You've hardly eaten anything from our stores."

Zamna shrugged. "My tastes are different from yours." He hissed slightly with laughter.

As they passed by one of the farms, Taren noticed livestock in the fields. Moving closer, he could clearly see the soft white fleece of sheep. His master's words echoed in his mind: "Head south through the woods until the wool looks strange, and then continue until it's normal again." This wool was certainly more normal than the red fleece of the Rixville sheep.

Turning to his companion, Taren said, "We must be getting close."

"How can you tell?" Zamna wondered.

"My master said the wool would be normal when I was nearing the tomb."

Zamna looked over at the sheep and asked, "Is that normal to you?"

Taren seemed confused. "Yes, it is," he replied. "What does a La'kertan sheep look like?"

Laughing, he replied, "There's no such animal in my homeland. The only sheep I've encountered were those red ones. I didn't know there were different varieties."

"I didn't either," Taren admitted. "I only know what my master meant. In Ky'sall, the sheep look like these." He pointed to the field, wondering if there was any significance to the wool or if Imrit had simply used them as a visual aid.

Continuing past the farms, they moved at a good pace. There were no obstacles on the ground, and the weather was still beautiful. After several hours, they came across a dirt road leading east-west. It was poorly tended, likely being used only at harvest time.

Looking westward, Zamna asked, "Does that map of yours mention how far the towns might be? I'd be willing to take a short detour for an ale."

The mage shook his head. "Master Imrit copied this map from a centuries-old text. None of the cities are listed, only landscapes. I don't believe it's drawn to scale either, and it doesn't seem to reflect the changes that have occurred to the land over the centuries."

Zamna sighed with disappointment. "We might as well keep going then," he said.

"We could ask one of the farmers," Taren suggested.

"No," Zamna replied. "Let's keep moving. If you're right and we're near the tomb, then soon I'll be able to purchase the whole tavern rather than one drink." Grinning at his companion, he clapped him on the shoulder before setting off.

The two walked side by side, enjoying the soft grass underfoot. The next day would bring yet another change to the land. Ahead in the distance, they could see that the grass was about to come to an end. A distinct line of demarcation brought an end to the prairie as if a wall separated the two areas. The ground before them was a pale red-brown. Taren knelt to feel the soil, which slipped through his fingers like dust.

"This land is dead," he stated. "There are no nutrients in this soil." Looking back over his shoulder, he longed for the grassland they had just crossed. The way ahead felt ominous and uninviting.

Zamna looked back at the grass as well. "I think that curse sort of comes and goes," he said, referring to the Sisters' warning.

"It seems that way," Taren agreed. "Though, I suppose we haven't seen every detail of those lands. They all might be cursed in one way or another."

Turning to face the barren land ahead of them, Zamna said, "This land feels cursed, no doubt about it. I'm not a man to stand in fear, but I have no desire to enter this place." He stared ahead into the desolate region before him and frowned.

"You aren't obligated to accompany me," Taren said. "I have no choice, but you are welcome to leave if you want to." Taren hoped the La'kertan would choose to continue their journey. So far, he had proved a useful companion, and spending who knows how long alone in the bleak land ahead would likely weaken his resolve to continue.

Zamna stared at him in disbelief. "Have I found this treasure I'm after? If I turn back now, I get nothing." He shook his head. "I promised to accompany you to this tomb, and I have yet to set foot inside it. I'm going in there, like it or not."

Taren's lips curled into a smile. With a nod, he stepped forward, placing his feet firmly on the lifeless soil. There were no trees to be seen, no grass, and no wildlife, not even insects. Whatever had happened to this land, it had destroyed life in the area absolutely. If ever they had set foot in a cursed land, this was surely it. The lands they had traversed previously had their quirks, but this one was the worst of all.

Taren had been given no warning about this place, but it reminded him slightly of The Barrens near his home. He found himself constantly turning his head in search of the strange stone beast that had attacked the other two apprentices. Though he dreaded the thought of someday returning to that land, the area he was currently walking through felt much worse. He had witnessed no death here, but he could feel it all around him. His heart thumped loudly in his ears, his chest visibly rising and falling with each breath.

Zamna felt uneasy as well. He carried a dagger in his hand rather than allowing it to rest in its sheath, as it had for most of the journey. Though there was no sign of life, he expected an attack at any moment. This land was strange, and every one of his senses was on high alert.

They trudged on, neither man saying a word. Their ears attuned to their surroundings, listening intently for the slightest sign of life. As the day wore on, the sky took on a deep-red haze.

"Are those clouds?" the La'kertan wondered aloud.

Taren had no idea. "Let's hope that's all they are."

The sky drew darker as they traveled, and an occasional pecking sound made its way to their ears. Exchanging puzzled glances, they listened more closely, hoping to determine what was making the noise.

Zamna's eyes caught sight of tiny objects dropping ahead of them in the distance. "I think it's raining," he said.

The sounds continued, becoming more numerous and more frequent. The raindrops reached their location, hitting them heavily as they fell. Observing the ground at their feet, they noticed the raindrops did not soak into the soil. Instead, they remained on top, laying where they fell.

Taren knelt down and reached out a hand to the object that fell from the sky. Turning it over in his hand, he stood upright and handed the item to his companion. "It's not rain," he declared. "These are bone fragments."

Taking the object, Zamna shuddered. It was small, but unmistakably, a piece of dried bone. It was pitted at the center where the marrow had once been. What caused these bones to fall from the sky he could not say. In all his travels, he had never encountered anything so strange.

The bones continued to fall, the shower becoming more intense. The fragments grew larger, and the men lifted their packs above their heads to shield themselves from the downpour. Eventually, entire bones dropped to the ground, some resembling human parts, others animal, and some of them were completely unknown to the travelers.

They dashed through the deluge, hoping to make it to shelter. In the distance, they spotted an old barn, the dilapidated structure barely standing.

"It looks like it's about to fall down," Taren said as they moved closer to the building.

"It's still better than being pummeled by bones," Zamna replied.

The two men ran inside and lowered their packs, the sound of the rain pounding against the top of the barn. There were numerous holes in the roof, but the fragments were too large to fit through. The boards composing the structure creaked slightly as the storm continued.

"Do you have a spell that will fortify this barn?" Zamna asked. "I'm not sure how long it's been standing, but it doesn't look good."

Zamna was correct. The wooden structure had stood in disrepair since the land fell under Ailwen's power. It was composed only of wooden slats, which had avoided rot only due to the absence of moisture in this land. Still the lack of care had resulted in loose boards and a weakened frame. The entire building moved slightly under the weight of the bones.

"I can try," Taren replied. Digging into his magical knowledge, he tried to find the correct spell to stop the barn from collapsing on top of them. Deciding on an appropriate spell, he rose and placed his hands against the nearest wall. Spreading white magic from his hands, he repeated the spell on each of the four walls before blasting the magic toward the ceiling. "That should help," he declared.

The two men settled in to wait out the storm. With travel impossible, they decided to try to rest for the journey ahead. They had no idea how much ground there still was to cover, so they might as well rest while they had the chance. The sound of the rain became lighter, returning to the smaller chunks of bone that had fallen at first, but it refused to stop. It continued on for hours, the bones piling up outside the opening to the barn.

"It's going to be awkward walking through that," Zamna said with a sigh.

Taren feared the La'kertan might be right. The land was completely covered, and the bones were still coming down. Wading through them might soon become impossible. Reaching out into the rain, he collected a handful of fragments to fashion into a small fire. Though it was not cold in this land, fire provided a peaceful feeling of home, and he longed for its comfort.

As the blue magical flames roared to life, the two men spread out their beds on either side of the fire. Neither of them were tired, and both felt uneasy about the land they were in.

Taren could bear the silence no longer. Propping himself up on his elbow, he said, "Tell me about La'kerta."

Zamna looked at him curiously but remained silent.

"Why did you leave there?" Taren wondered, finally not too nervous to ask. He had traveled for weeks with this man about whom he still knew so little. Curiosity finally got the better of him, and he would press on until he knew the La'kertan's story. "Tell me how you ended up an assassin. Did someone train you or did you learn on your own?"

Zamna settled back against his bed and stared up at the wooden ceiling. With a sigh, he said, "La'kerta is an island filled with dense jungles. There are few visitors to be found, and my people keep mainly to themselves. My family was dirt poor, living on what the jungle itself could provide."

"Are there no cities?" Taren wondered.

"There are," Zamna replied. "But my family did not travel to them. There is corruption and fighting in the cities, and they preferred to stay in the jungle."

"Is that why you left?" Taren asked. "Were you tired of living that way?"

"I knew there was a bigger world out there that I was missing out on. I yearned to explore other lands from the time I was a child. One day, I just decided to go."

"Alone? Were you frightened?"

"I wasn't smart enough to be frightened," he said with a laugh. "I was young and sure of myself. I worked my way onto ships, mostly cleaning up after the sailors. They weren't too happy to have me around, but I managed. I visited lands full of humans and elves, and I haven't returned home since."

"How did you become an assassin?" This was the most pressing question Taren had for his friend. The La'kertan did not strike him as a killer, yet that was the profession he had chosen. There must be a reason.

"I wanted to be rich," he began. "Unfortunately, everywhere I went, people looked down on me and treated me like dirt. The only jobs I could find involved cleaning up after animals and other manual labor that humans are loathe to do. They wouldn't consider allowing me to work alongside them in any respectable position. I finally tired of it and took to the streets. I'll spare you the sad story there."

"But you got off the streets," Taren said. "You found work as an assassin." He was still interested in hearing more of the story, and he had no intention of dropping the subject.

With a sigh, Zamna continued. "Let's just say when you live on the streets, you have to learn to steal. Then you have to learn to defend yourself against those who would steal what you've already stolen. It's a vicious way of life, and only those who are willing to do what it takes will survive."

Taren wasn't sure he wanted the details of that way of life. It would seem his friend had been forced into killing from a young age. Life on the streets had to have been brutal.

Before the mage could press him further, Zamna chose to continue his story. "One day, I saw a man in a black cloak who was wearing a jeweled ring on every finger of his right hand. I stole three of those rings before he realized I was there. He was angry but impressed with my abilities. He introduced me to his friends, a group of highly skilled assassins. I spent the next few years training to become one of them, and I've been doing that work ever since."

Taren understood. A life of hardship had led him to become what he was. There was only one question that remained. "If you find treasure in Ailwen's tomb, will you continue on in your profession?"

Without hesitation, he replied, "If there is treasure in that tomb, I'll never need to take another job. I'll find someplace to settle down and enjoy my wealth."

Pleased by his friend's response, Taren smiled. "Then I hope there is treasure beyond your wildest dreams." The man next to him was not a hardened criminal who killed people for pleasure. He had been a frightened child alone in a world that refused to accept him. He had done what was necessary to survive. Taren respected his desire to move on to a better life. If he could help his friend accomplish his goal, he would. Zamna was free to take any and all riches inside the tomb, with the sole exception being the magical symbol Taren sought for his master.

Chapter 15

The rain of bones ended sometime in the night as the travelers slept soundly in their shelter. Taren awoke first and looked out into the morning sunlight. To his amazement, all of the bone fragments had completely disappeared, leaving no trace of their presence behind. Taren stepped outside the wooden structure to have a better look at the land. Everywhere he looked, the ground was clear of debris. All that remained was the same red-brown dirt that had been there before.

Stepping back inside, he saw that Zamna was awake and sitting up on his bed. He stretched his limbs and cracked his knuckles before nodding to his companion.

"You'll never believe it," Taren said. "The bones are gone."

Puzzled, Zamna pulled himself to his feet and stepped outside. The mage had spoken correctly. There was no debris. Stepping back inside, he said, "I guess we won't have to climb over mountains of bones today."

They shared a few rations for breakfast before packing up their gear. Both men hoped the rain would stay away this day. They were anxious to get moving, hoping that they would arrive at the tomb soon.

"Did that master of yours say how we'll recognize this tomb?" Zamna asked. "There could be dozens of graves in this land."

"Unfortunately he did not," Taren replied. "Ailwen was an incredibly powerful sorceress. I don't think her remains will lie in a common tomb. I'd expect it to be something impressive."

They marched on until midday, when a large building came into view. Pausing, they stared toward the horizon, taking in the sight before them. The building was crafted of white stone that shone brightly beneath the sunlight. Exchanging glances, the two men moved closer for a better look.

As they approached, they realized this was not one single building. It was a massive compound. Dozens of buildings of varying sizes stood tall in the distance. Each was crafted from the same white stones, which showed obvious signs of wear and neglect.

"Is this a city?" Zamna asked.

Taren didn't think so. "This has to be what we're looking for," he said, pulling his map from his bag. "If it were a city, it would not be so weather worn." Every city they had encountered so far had not appeared on his map because the map had been drafted long before those cities existed. As his eyes pored over the structures before him, he could plainly see that it was ancient. The domed-roof architecture had not been employed for a millennium, and the crumbling walls suggested their advanced age. "This must be where the sorceress lived before she destroyed herself and left a curse on the land. Her actual tomb has to be somewhere inside."

"Which building do we go in?" Zamna wondered. There were several small buildings, as well as a few large ones, all of which were connected by a series of stone corridors. Finding the tomb could take days if they had to search each building. "Do you have a map of the inside?"

Taren shook his head. An interior map was a luxury he wished he possessed. "I think we should go in the center structure," Taren said, pointing at the large building standing at the front of the compound. "All of the buildings are connected, so we might as well start front and center."

Zamna shrugged. It was as good a plan as any. They marched on, finally coming face to face with the stone door where they hoped to gain entry. At its center, it bore a large, round stone engraved with hundreds of runic symbols.

Taren placed his fingers on the stone, feeling the lines of the carvings. They were rough and cool to the touch, but the runes were still readable. Unfortunately, he did not recognize some of the symbols. The writing appeared to be gibberish. "Some of these runes make no sense," Taren said.

"Maybe the ancient dialect was different from what you've studied," Zamna suggested. None of the runes were familiar to the assassin. If Taren couldn't read them, he hoped deciphering them wasn't necessary to gain entry.

Taren shook his head. "Magic hasn't changed," he stated. "There's something different about the runes, though."

"Does it matter?" Zamna asked impatiently. "Can we get inside without reading the door?"

Taren pressed his hand against the stone entrance, but it did not budge. Zamna approached and shoved his full weight against it, but still it held fast.

"Maybe the symbols tell us how to open it," Taren said.

Zamna sighed and took a seat near the door. "Then it's up to you," he declared. "I can't read it, and I can't perform any magic on it. If all else fails, try blasting it open."

"I'd rather not damage anything if I can avoid it," he replied. "Anyway, I'm not sure I know a spell strong enough to blast through the thick stone." He ran his hand along the rough stone surface of the door. Its composition was strange to him, as if it had been crafted from an unknown mineral. Mostly gray in color, it had a strange sheen to it despite its weathered exterior. Seemingly impenetrable, he saw no cracks or other signs of weakness.

"If only I had my books with me," Taren said with a sigh. "Maybe I could figure out what this says."

"Take your time," Zamna said. "You'll figure it out." Hoping Taren just needed some time to solve the puzzle, he settled in with his back against the stone wall. He was confident in the mage's abilities and hoped it would not be long before they were inside.

Taren studied the runes closely, still unsure how to proceed. After an hour, he realized that most of the words referred to spells from the four schools of magic. The spells varied in the level of difficulty as they approached the center of the stone. Seemingly, they were in no particular order. Different schools were placed next to each other, and there appeared to be no pattern involved in their positioning. The spells did not build or complement each other, and he had no idea which one he should cast, if any.

"You still have no idea?" Zamna asked, growing impatient. He had hoped to be inside by now. If Taren couldn't figure out how to get inside, their journey would be nothing more than a waste of time. "Maybe we should try a different door," he suggested.

"Maybe," Taren said, scratching his head.

Zamna hopped up and led the way as the pair attempted to circle the grounds. They approached the nearest building, but to their dismay, it had no door, window, or other visible means of entry. Moving on, they inspected a third and then a fourth building. None of them revealed a path inside. Even the corridors between each structure were completely enclosed with no openings at all.

"Not even a window?" Zamna said in disbelief. "What kind of place is this? The people who lived here encased themselves in stone?" He couldn't imagine living in such a way. Being eternally confined within stone might as well be death.

"There aren't too many records of Ailwen's time," Taren said. "Master Imrit found what he could, but there was no explanation of how to get inside."

"We might as well go back to the front," Zamna said, frustrated by the situation. "At least we found some sort of door. Try blasting it with your magic."

Taren agreed and followed his companion back to the runed door. Summoning his magic, he blasted energy at the door. It stood unfazed. Trying again, he sent a second energy burst, this time more intense. Nothing. The door held fast, refusing to allow the pair entry.

Zamna shook his head and sat once again, his arms resting on his knees. "We'll just have to wait until you figure it out, I suppose." He was quickly losing faith in his companion, but he would wait as long as he could stand it. Getting into the tomb was his only chance at retrieving the riches inside, and he hadn't traveled this far to go away empty handed.

This time when Taren observed the runes, a zigzagged line stood out to him. All of the spells along that line belonged to the school of earth magic. Maybe all he needed to do was cast each spell consecutively, using the door as his target. "I have an idea," he announced to his companion.

Zamna did not speak. Instead, he raised his eye ridges and waited to see what the mage was going to do. Taren moved away from the door a few steps and focused his energy on the first spell. The corresponding runes glowed with a green light as the spell hit its target. Moving on, he cast the second spell, causing those runes to glow. As he moved to the third spell, he noticed that the first set of runes had stopped glowing, and the second set was fading. When the magic reached the door, only the corresponding set of runes remained alight. In earnest, he continued casting each spell in turn, hoping that when he came to the last one, all of the runes would light up and the door would unlock. Unfortunately, that was not to be the case. Once he had finished casting the final spell, only the matching runes were lit. After a moment, the color faded away, leaving the wall as it had been before. The door was still locked.

Taren growled low in his throat, annoyed that his idea had not worked. How was he supposed to open the door if the answer would not show itself? Staring intently at the runes, he strained his eyes to the point of pain. He simply could not see the solution to this puzzle.

Searching along the etchings, he found another line of zigzagging spells, all from the school of air magic. Though it was not his specialty, he felt he would be able to cast each of those particular spells. Taking a few deep breaths to center himself, he tapped into his magical stores for a second try. The runes flashed with silver light as the magic touched the door, and Taren felt a spark of hope. Concentrating on the second spell, it too lit the correct runes, but the first set of runes had already gone out. Determined not to give up, he continued each incantation until he came to the end. Waiting with bated breath, he stood expecting the door to open. It did not.

Taren searched his memory for any trace of a clue as to how to get inside the tomb. The only words that came to mind were Zamna's. In his travels, he had heard little about the tomb, but what he had said stuck

241

in Taren's mind. If the door could be opened only by a true master of the arcane as Zamna had suggested, then Taren would likely need to cast spells from all the schools. Studying the runes again, he searched for a similar zigzagging line of fire or water magic.

After several minutes, he found such a line of fire spells. It was not the exact same pattern as earth or air, but it would have to do. As he studied each of the runic symbols, he realized that three of them corresponded with spells that were not familiar to him. Had he been a master of fire, it was possible he could have cast them with ease. Was this why Imrit had sent all three of them? Did he know more than he had revealed? Or did he simply wish to cover all the bases? Taren could not be sure. All he could do was wish that his fellow apprentices had not perished in The Barrens. Their deaths were senseless wastes. Tissa and Djo deserved to be here beside him to unlock the secrets held within this tomb.

With his last ounce of hope remaining, he searched the runes for water spells. The result was the same. An even more random zigzagging line presented him with seven water spells he could not possibly cast. Two of them contained runic symbols he had never seen, rendering them completely meaningless. Staring in disbelief, he forced himself to admit that he lacked the skills to get them inside the tomb.

"I can't do it," he said, placing his head in his hands. "I've failed." Sitting down heavily next to Zamna, he felt the heat rising into his face. A lifetime of work had led him to a dead end, and he would never be able to retrieve the symbol for his aged master. Wishing he had died in The Barrens and saved himself the agony of this defeat, the tears crept into his eyes.

With his voice perfectly calm, Zamna asked, "What does this tomb mean to you?"

Taren wiped his eyes on his sleeve and looked out at the horizon. "It means immortality for my master," he admitted. His mind filled with images of the elderly wizard, hard at work in his laboratory. Taren realized he would never see him again. How could he possibly return and tell him he had failed? No, he would not do it.

"I don't know this master of yours," Zamna replied, "but I do know that you admire him greatly." He turned to look at the young mage. "If he means so much to you, giving up isn't an option. I can see that you're frustrated, but it was never supposed to be easy to get inside." He sighed. "I hoped it would be. I hoped you'd have that door open in a matter of minutes, and we'd be finished by sundown." He too looked out over the horizon where the sun was setting, and the sky was filling with a soft orange light. "That just isn't how things work out. You've been reading too many fairy tales if you thought you'd get here and everything would magically work out the way it was supposed to." Hissing softly with laughter, he patted his friend on the back. "Maybe we should get some rest. You can look on it with fresh eyes in the morning."

Despite all his quirks, Zamna's words held wisdom. The La'kertan was not the sort of man to sugarcoat things or lie to make someone else feel better. Obviously, he had true confidence in him, and that made Taren hopeful once more. If his companion believed in him, it was time he started believing in himself.

Leaning his back to the wall, he stared at the sky above. There were three moons present in the sky, each of them overlapping the one next to it. Ruffling his brow, he pointed to the moons and asked, "Have you ever seen that before?"

The La'kertan shook his head. "In all my travels, I've seen only one moon at a time."

Taren continued to observe the moons. How could they possibly have changed? Could it be a result of the curse on this land? Maybe it was a sign of some kind. Perhaps he needed to cast magic from only three different schools. Shaking off the idea, he realized it didn't make sense. Why only three schools when there were four to choose from?

With his stomach beginning to rumble, he decided to have a bite to eat. The pair shared a few rations of nuts and fruit, their supplies of which were becoming quite low. It was unlikely they would find anything to hunt in this land, and there was little chance of finding food inside the tomb, if they ever got inside. All that remained were the ingredients Taren had harvested in the meadow, and the potions he had crafted before leaving home. Some of them could indeed take the place of food in an emergency. Content that he at least had enough to get them to the nearest town, he unrolled his bed and lay down. Potions were something he could do correctly. If only he could use them on the entrance. Sadly, he had never heard of a potion that could unlock a door.

Chapter 16

Sleep eluded Taren, so instead of sleeping he silently
stared up at the night sky, searching for familiar
constellations. To his surprise, the stars in this land did
not resemble those of his home. Here there were no
familiar arrangements to the stars, and it puzzled him.
As the sky grew darker and more stars appeared in the
sky, he became ever more certain that he was correct.
He felt like he had been transported to another world.

With the pattern of the alien stars embedded in his
mind, he finally drifted off to sleep. Swirling patterns
of color appeared before his sleeping eyes. Shades of
red and green swirled themselves against a black
background. Out of nowhere, bright-silver dots
appeared through the black, some of them far brighter
than others. They formed a shape that was unknown

to him, but he was certain it was some sort of runic symbol. The lines crossed over themselves, connecting the brightest lights while the colors continued to swirl. He awoke with a start, his mind more confused than ever.

Zamna was already awake beside him, sitting cross-legged near the white-stone wall. "Good morning," he said. "Ready to try again?" Grinning at his friend, he gestured his thumb at the door.

To Taren's disappointment, the door had not magically opened itself in the night. That would have been far too convenient. With a sigh, he lifted himself from his bed and approached the rune carvings. Looking back at Zamna, his face revealed his uncertainty.

"Just take a deep breath and try anything," the La'kertan suggested. "It will come to you." Staying positive was becoming increasingly hard for the assassin. It wasn't exactly in his nature to be encouraging and supportive. However, if acting in that way would get him inside the tomb, he would give it a try.

Flashing in the mage's mind was an image of the constellation he had seen in his dream. An idea occurred to him. What if he cast spells that took up the same positions as the stars in that formation? Hungrily, his eyes scanned the runes for the pattern. It was only a moment before he found it. Unfortunately, he could not cast all of the spells that appeared before him. Hoping he could find the pattern among a different set of runes, he continued to scan the engravings. Indeed he found what he needed. There were several instances of the exact same pattern, but only one of those contained spells he was confident in casting. They came from the schools of earth, air, and fire, which would account for the green, silver, and red he had seen in his dream. Flashing a smile to his companion, he focused his energy on his magic.

Reaching deep into his stores, he cast the first spell at the door, and the corresponding runes lit up. As he began the second spell, the first set of runes grew dim, and the second set lit up. Taren wasn't sure if this was how it should be, so he continued along, casting each spell in turn. When he had finished, he waited for the door to open. A minute passed and then another. Nothing. Screaming in frustration he kicked the door and pounded on it with his fists.

Zamna sprang to his feet to restrain the aggravated mage. Pulling him away from the door, he said, "Calm down. You can do this. Try casting faster or slower, or something else. You're probably making this harder than it really is."

Taren took a deep breath and blew it out slowly. Zamna was probably right. Determined to try again, he looked back at the rune carvings. Another image flashed in his mind—the three moons he had seen overlapping the night before. Could that be the answer? If he started the second spell before the first was completed, the magic would overlap. His breath came heavier as he searched his mind, wondering if he was capable of such magic. It took a great deal of concentration to cast a single spell. How could he split his mind and cast two simultaneously?

Resolving to try it, he stood firm before the door. Closing his eyes, he began to take deep breaths, each time increasing the length of his exhale. When he felt himself perfectly calm, he dug into the stores of magic remaining to him. With a focused mind, he cast the first spell and held it as his right hand blasted red magic against the stone door. The first set of runes lit with a red light. Holding onto his composure, he began the second spell while still holding the first. Green magic flew from the fingers of his left hand, landing against the door. The second set of runes glowed green, while the first set remained lit as well.

Taren did not let this success interrupt his concentration. Stopping to be amazed by this feat would have only resulted in another failure. Staying focused, he ended the first spell and cast the third while still holding the second. Success. The three runes lit themselves, sparkling bright with magical energy. The young mage continued in this manner, maintaining his focus until he reached the last spell. Before his eyes, the line of runes glowed brightly in a perfect imitation of the constellation he had seen in his dream.

Both men stared as the runes continued to glow, increasing in their intensity. Taren felt weary and drained, but he remained on his feet. A rumbling sound erupted from beneath their feet as the massive stone carving began to move. It spun itself in a circular pattern before slipping down inside the door. The door itself began to shake, dust and debris that had lain dormant for centuries falling from its edges. As if in slow motion, the door sank down into the ground, disappearing before their eyes. A dark corridor beckoned them inside.

Amazed by what had just occurred, Taren said, "Only a master wizard can cast two spells at once."

His voice was hollow, the young mage still in shock at what he had done.

Zamna replied, "Congratulations, Master. It looks like you've passed the test."

Overcome by weariness, Taren buckled to his knees. Zamna rushed to his side, stopping him from falling face down on the stone floor.

"You need to take one of your potions," Zamna said. Grabbing the mage's pack, he opened it and looked inside. "Which one is it?"

Taren sat and reached out for the bag. Pulling out a rejuvenation potion, he hesitated before putting it to his lips.

"Drink," the La'kertan demanded. "We're going inside now. You need your strength, and we don't have days to wait."

The mage downed the entire potion at once, feeling its energizing effects throughout his body. If this was the end of the journey, it would not matter if he ran out. All that was left was to reach Ailwen's final resting place and retrieve the symbol that was likely still clutched in her grip.

Standing outside the open door, the two men peered into the dark corridor. The air inside the stone structure was cold and still. Taren placed an arm across his companion's path, preventing him from stepping forward.

"Let me cast a spell to detect any traps," he said.

Zamna nodded his agreement as the mage focused his energy to the spell. He saw nothing ahead, but to his amazement, a series of lamps lit themselves along the walls.

"Did you do that?" Zamna asked.

"I'm not sure," the mage replied. "That wasn't the spell I cast, but the building seems to have used my magic to illuminate the passage ahead."

As they moved forward, the lights behind them dimmed while the lights in front of them grew brighter. Because the building had been constructed through magic, it held onto the power unleashed by the young mage, and recycled it as he passed through its halls.

Entering the first room, their eyes fell on a pile of bones on the stone floor. As they watched, it began to take shape, forming itself into a complete skeleton. Zamna readied his daggers, preparing himself for an attack. Taren stood perfectly still, staring at the figure ahead. The bleached white skull still had rotten bits of yellowed flesh attached to it, and it wore a dark hood. Instantly Taren recognized it from the vision he had in the crystal cave. The image of death stood before them.

The skeletal form raised its hand, halting the two of them from taking action. It creaked as it moved forward, approaching the pair slowly. Small plumes of dust released from its joints as it walked, and Taren marveled at its ability to hold itself together.

Zamna remained at the ready but did not strike. Waiting to see if the skeleton was friend or foe, he held his weapons steady. Whispering to Taren, he asked, "Didn't the Sisters say that bones were an omen of good fortune?"

Taren nodded, watching carefully as the skeleton approached. Its mouth hung open in an unnatural way, giving it the appearance that it was screaming, though no sound was being produced. Closer and closer it marched, until finally it came face to face with the travelers.

"I will lead you to the Mistress's tomb," it said in a low, raspy voice.

Taren and Zamna exchanged glances. "Why would you do that?" Zamna asked.

The skeleton slanted its skull to the La'kertan, staring at him with empty eye sockets. "I am bidden to do so," it said.

"Do you have a name?" the mage asked.

The skeleton shook its head.

"What do we call him, then?" Zamna asked. "Bone Man?"

Ignoring the comment, Taren asked, "How far is it to the tomb?"

"This fortress is a maze of intersecting corridors and rooms," the skeleton explained. "You will die alone if you do not follow me." Saying nothing else, it turned its bony back to them and walked away.

The pair hesitated momentarily before following. Exchanging glances, they silently agreed to trust in the wisdom of the Sisters of Gy'dan. Slowly they followed the bone man as he moved along the passage. Shapes and shadows shifted at the corners of their eyes, causing them to jerk their heads from side to side. All was silent, suggesting the shadows were nothing more than their imagination. Any creature moving about in this stillness would surely be heard.

Soon the trio came to the entrance of a wide, empty room. A single pillar of stone stood at the center of the room, a glowing gem of green affixed to its pointed top. As they stepped inside, the gem began to spin, emitting a green beam of light. The light scanned each of the travelers, remaining the longest on Taren.

Without warning, the pillar fired upon them, knocking both the La'kertan and the mage to the ground. The bone man remained unaffected. He stood as solid as ever, waiting for the men to rejoin him.

Zamna jumped to his feet but was struck by a second blast from the pillar. It knocked him back, this time sending him sprawling against the wall. Taren scrambled to his feet, narrowly missing a green blast that was intended for him.

Dropping to his knees at Zamna's side, he asked, "Are you all right?"

The La'kertan nodded but stayed down. "How do we get past it?"

Not knowing what name to use for the skeleton, Taren called out, "Why is this thing attacking us?"

The bone man did not reply. Maintaining his silence, he stood at the far side of the room and waited. This matter did not involve him. If they wished to visit the tomb, they must deal with the obstacles on their own. He would guide them through the passages, but he would neither fight nor provide any other assistance.

"It doesn't seem to fire when we're down," Taren said. "My guess is it doesn't want to kill us."

"Maybe the trigger is on the level with the gemstone," Zamna suggested. "It's about the level of our heads."

"Are you suggesting we crawl across the floor to avoid it?" Taren asked.

Zamna shrugged. "It's worth a try."

Zamna rolled onto his belly, and Taren dropped lower to the ground. Slowly they crawled across the floor, their hands grasping at the dust of centuries that coated the stone floor. The pillar at the center of the room flashed a few times but did not fire upon them. Remaining low to the ground, they exited into the corridor ahead. The skeleton led on, walking at an easy pace along the path.

"That wasn't so bad," Taren commented.

Zamna said nothing. Whatever that pillar was, he was certain it wasn't intended to kill. It had hit him with two separate blasts, which had only hindered him. If it wanted to kill him, it was going about it the wrong way. It was simply an ancient device of forgotten design. He hoped the next room would not contain a stronger one.

They pressed on down the corridor, eventually coming to a second room. This one was also empty, but its ceiling was lower. The left-hand side of the floor was tilted upward. Moving forward, the bone man encountered no problems. However, when Taren and Zamna stepped inside, the floor shifted, knocking them off-balance. They rolled across the ground to the right, the floor sinking under the weight. As they struggled back to their feet, the ceiling shifted. It came down close to their heads, forcing them to throw their hands up to stop it.

"How did he get across?" Taren asked, looking at the bone man.

"It wasn't designed to keep him out," Zamna replied. Whoever built this place obviously did not want visitors. "I'll hold this end while you move toward the exit. Then you can hold up that end for me."

Nodding his understanding, Taren moved forward, taking careful steps to avoid disturbing the balance further. As he reached the far end, he stretched himself between the floor and ceiling, and awaited the arrival of his companion.

Zamna walked in a crouched position, each step landing softly against the unstable floor. Arriving at his companion's side, he said, "Now we need to make a dash for it."

"On three," Taren said, still holding up the edge of the ceiling. "One…two…three!" Dropping his arms, he ran to the exit with Zamna on his heels.

The moment they reached the doorway, the ceiling and floor came together with a thunderous clap. The opposite end of the room reacted with its own crash as the two slabs were forced together.

"That would have smashed us like ants," Taren commented, staring back at the slabs. "Why didn't you warn us?" Stepping close to the skeleton, he awaited a response.

His question was met with silence. Without a word, the bone man turned his back to the travelers and led them deeper inside the compound.

"Are you sure we can trust him?" Zamna asked.

Taren shook his head. He had only the word of the Sisters to go by. This was definitely the same creature he had seen in his vision. If they believed him to be a sign of good, that meant he would lead them to their final destination. "We don't have much choice," he said. "Without him we'd be wandering here for days or longer. There might be far worse traps if we stray from the correct route."

Zamna grumbled under his breath but kept his comments to himself. The mage made a valid point, but he was still wary of trusting a creature who would not offer any warning of the danger ahead. Of course they had entered expecting danger, so it was reasonable to assume there would be plenty of it. The only thing lacking was treasure. How long had they been inside? There had been no sign of anything gold or silver. Stone, dust, and bones were all they'd seen so far. If Ailwen's tomb contained no treasure, he would take out his frustrations on the bone man. The thought brought a smile to his scaly lips.

Chapter 17

The skeletal figure led them down a long passage, turning several times as the intersecting tunnels meandered along their way. It proved impossible for the companions to keep their bearings as they marched along, ever watching for the next obstacle in their path. The bone man walked on in silence, having spoken no words since their first encounter near the entrance. Only the sound of his creaking bones and the footsteps of the travelers filled the emptiness of the forgotten compound. Somewhere ahead lay the remains of the most reviled sorceress of her time. Mostly forgotten, no others had an interest in visiting this remote location. Thoughts of the symbol filled Taren's mind as he sensed himself moving closer and closer to completing his goal.

Finally their path wound through to another room, this one lacking the stone floor they had become accustomed to. Instead, the ground was covered in a soft, black soil, and the walls appeared slick and wet. Vibrantly colored mushrooms grew in perfectly ordered rows, thriving in the darkness that normally filled this space. Taren's recycled magic illuminated the room, bringing light to plants that had likely never been exposed to it.

Taren had never seen such colorful mushrooms before. They seemed to glow with an unearthly light, and in nature, fluorescent-colored things usually meant trouble. Though he had no intention of eating one, he took a moment to examine the fungi more closely. The bone man waited patiently at the exit, still not saying a word. Taren leaned down next to a bundle of mushrooms and inhaled. They smelled of nothing except freshly tended earth. In fact, the scent was appealing. It almost made him want to taste them.

Zamna came to his side with a warning. "I wouldn't touch those," he said. "Everything else here has tried to harm or kill us. These likely aren't any different."

Nodding his agreement, the mage said, "I bet whoever put these here hoped we'd be hungry after our long walk and take a bite. There's little chance these are not poisonous."

"Probably the most poisonous substance in all Nōl'Deron," Zamna commented. Realizing what he'd just said, he thought the mushrooms could prove an excellent tool for an assassin. He nearly asked if there might be harm in taking a few before remembering that his days in that line of work were nearly at an end. Once they reached the burial site, he hoped to find treasure enough to allow him to retire. No more killing meant no more poisoning.

"I'd like to take a few for study," Taren said. "Though, I'm not sure I want to touch them." As he looked more closely, he saw tiny beads of a milky substance on the caps of the mushrooms. Clearly they were poisonous, possibly lethal to the touch. Deciding it was best to leave them alone, he rose and rejoined his skeleton guide.

Moving out into the corridor, Zamna said, "Hey, at least nothing jumped out to grab us in there." He hissed softly with laughter.

Taren chuckled a little as well. There had been no odd mushroom beast, angry that they were invading his farm. No menacing gnomes had threatened them for entering their garden. So far, the mushroom area had proved the least deadly of the non-empty rooms they'd passed through.

Turning sharply to the left, the corridor led them into a tiny room with no obvious signs of traps. Barely larger than a closet, it held nothing except dust. Continuing along their way, they entered another tunnel, this time turning off to the right. After several minutes, they wondered when they would emerge on the other side. This had to be the longest corridor they had entered thus far. The lamps along the wall did not illuminate far enough ahead to see the end, and Taren was starting to worry. To his relief, a few minutes more brought them to an opening.

A vast room spread out before them, empty except for a stone pillar at its center. The two men instinctively lowered themselves, crouching near the ground and bracing themselves for a blast of magic. No such attack came, though. The two men dared to stand upright, facing the pillar. At first glance, Taren was sure he would have to dodge a sudden attack. Further observation, however, showed him otherwise. The top of the pillar had crumbled over time, and it was no longer sturdy enough to house the gemstone. Instead, the sparkling blue gem lay on the floor, half covered with debris.

Zamna's eye fell on the sparkling sapphire. "Looks like our luck is changing," he commented with a grin. Finally he might get his hands on something valuable.

"Indeed," Taren agreed. "This pillar probably would have tried to drown us. That is, if it had been in working condition." He strode forward boldly to examine the worn surface of the pillar. It appeared that a chunk of ceiling had fallen from above and crashed onto the pillar at some point. It was sturdy at the base but too weak at its narrow top to withstand such a blow. The area that once held the gem had been obliterated.

Zamna stepped forward cautiously and knelt down next to the pillar. Brushing away the crumbled stones, he retrieved the gem. After wiping the dust on his pants, he lifted the stone to his mouth and bit down. Though he couldn't speak for the quality, the hardness betrayed it as a genuine sapphire. Raising his eye ridges, he looked up at his companion. "You think Boney will mind if I take a souvenir?"

Taren shrugged and looked at their skeleton guide. He stood firm, facing away from the travelers. Still no words escaped his mouth. If he was upset by the theft, he certainly wasn't showing it. It appeared the stone was of no consequence to him.

Zamna tucked the precious gem into a pocket and motioned that he was ready to proceed. With the skeleton leading the way, they entered into a wide corridor, this one sloping downward as they continued on. The air became cooler and slightly damp, as if they had entered a cave. As the path proceeded lower, they realized they must now be underground.

Taren's heart was pounding in his ears, his anxiety rising. They must be extremely close now. He could almost feel the surface of the symbol in his hand. It could be in his grasp within minutes. Whispering to his companion, he asked, "Does it feel different in here to you?"

Zamna sniffed the air. "I think the air is staler," he replied. "It smells like rotting. There probably hasn't been a living person down here for hundreds of years." After a brief pause, he added, "It reminds me a little of that pit I was thrown in back in Yilde."

"What I meant was, do you sense anything?" Taren wondered if the symbol would cry out to anyone who was nearby, even if the person had no magical abilities.

"Like what?" Zamna wondered. "I don't get the feeling I'm being watched, if that's what you mean."

"A presence, a person, anything," Taren said. "I feel like we're nearly there."

Zamna shrugged. "You must have a sense I lack," he said. "If I could detect magic, I wouldn't have stepped on that trap and got myself into trouble." Though he did rely on intuition at times, he preferred to rely on the facts before him. Anything he could see, smell, or hear was important, and he made a point of taking in his surroundings at all times. An assassin always had to be on guard. This tomb felt empty and nothing more.

From the depths of the tomb, Taren could swear he heard the symbol crying out to him. Undisturbed for centuries, it would soon know life again. In the hands of Master Imrit, it would work incredible feats of magic. It had to be there, waiting for him ahead in the darkness.

Waiting patiently for someone to claim it, the symbol had locked its powers away. Taren could hold it in his hands this very day. All his thoughts focused on the symbol and how it would feel to finally retrieve it. How long would it take to return home? Would Imrit be able to sense it when the symbol was finally in the hands of his apprentice? Taren doubted it, but in secret, he hoped it was true. He could picture Imrit in his study, surrounded by books and scrolls. As the old man studied away, a notion would creep into his mind. He would behold a vision of Taren, symbol in hand. What pride the old man would feel in his apprentice. Young Taren, the boy he had practically raised, was now Master Taren.

Taren's reverie was broken by a small furry creature brushing against his leg. It let out a shrill shriek, and the mage nearly did as well. Turning to see what it was, he watched as a rat scurried past him, heading upward along the sloping corridor. Zamna flashed the young mage a grin, his spikey teeth glistening in the pale light.

The stone floor continued sloping downward, and the light grew dimmer as they descended lower into the earth. How far they had gone, Taren couldn't tell. The skeleton man said nothing, only continued along his way, never stopping or altering his pace. There was little choice but to follow until they reached the bottom.

Moving deeper along, a pungent smell emitted from below them. The skeletal guide was unfazed, but both Zamna and Taren grimaced at the horrible stench.

"Rotten eggs?" Taren asked.

"Maybe a poisonous gas," Zamna suggested. "Maybe it's a new way to try to get rid of us."

It was highly possible they would encounter another trap. Their long journey through the descending corridor had been so far uneventful. They felt overdue for an attack. Stepping more cautiously as they went, the duo was prepared for anything.

"We have to be getting close," Taren said. "I'd ask our guide, but he doesn't seem to be much of a talker."

"That's an understatement," Zamna replied. "Skeleton, are we almost out of this passageway?"

The skeleton said nothing. His creaking bones continued to move ahead, still sending up faint plumes of dust from time to time. Zamna shook his head. If he was truly leading them where they needed to go, then there was little need for him to speak. His guidance was enough in this vast labyrinth of stone structures. He had already saved them days of searching, so let him be silent if that was his desire.

After what seemed like an eternity, the path leveled off. An opening appeared before them, though it was not in the shape of a doorway like the others. This was a wide, irregular-shaped opening, similar to a cave mouth. The light became stronger again at this point, but soon it veered off, losing itself inside the massive room before them. It spread seemingly for miles in each direction. The yellow-tinged ceilings were adorned with giant stalactites wearing coats of shining white. They sparkled amid the dimly lit cavern, bringing beauty to the somber stillness inside.

Beneath their feet, the ground crunched audibly. It was coated in white as well, and tiny bits of mineral detached as their boots struck the ground. There were stalagmites of all size, ranging from one inch to several feet in length, though they were not as brightly colored as their counterparts on the ceiling. They wore a shade of tan upon the white, providing some variety to the room's décor. In some spots, the ceiling and floor connected with columns, most of them too wide for Taren to wrap his arms around. This place was indeed ancient, having formed when the world was still young. Stepping inside this cavern was like stepping into history and witnessing firsthand the beauty that lay trapped far below the feet of humans and elves.

Deeper in the cavern, they discovered large pools of a turquoise liquid that yellowed as they came in contact with the minerals surrounding it. This was the source of the smell they had first encountered in the passageway. The pools bubbled and steamed with no visible source of heat.

"Have you ever seen anything like that?" Zamna asked, staring into one of the pools.

Taren shook his head, not taking his eyes away from the liquid. "I suspect these are filled with sulfur, or some compound composed of it." He leaned down and held a hand above the pool, feeling the heat on his hand. "They must be heated by magma below us. This area is volcanic."

"Let's hope it doesn't plan to erupt any time soon," Zamna commented.

"I could be wrong," Taren said. "It's possible they have been exposed to some magic that heats them. I've never read about such pools existing inside a cave." Being in a cursed land meant that things were not necessarily as they seemed. In curiosity, he picked up a handful of small yellow rocks that had shaken loose from the ceiling and tossed them into the pool. In an instant, they vaporized, leaving no trace behind.

"We'd better watch our step," Zamna warned. "I wouldn't want to trip and land in that."

From the corner of his eye, Zamna spotted movement along the white cave floor. Camouflaged perfectly was a four-inch-long creature with a slender torso and elongated arms and legs. Moving in for a closer look, he realized its skin was translucent, and the veins inside its body were clearly visible.

Motioning for his companion to take a look, he marveled at the unique being before him.

"Is it an amphibian?" Taren asked, kneeling down next to it. In all his studies, he had never run across a creature quite like this.

Zamna shrugged. He moved no closer for fear of frightening the animal, though it seemed completely unbothered by his presence. Only once did it pause its motion and turn its head to one side. It had large, fanlike ears and a wide mouth, but no eyes could be seen on its face. Slowly it crept away from the pair, going about whatever business it had to do. The intruders in his home were of no interest.

Heading deeper inside the cavern, they beheld a network of swinging bridges where one could walk safely about the growing number of sulfur pools. The bone man led on, stopping abruptly as he reached the first bridge. The pair paused and exchanged glances, wondering why the skeleton had stopped.

"My duty is fulfilled," it said, its voice seeming to shrink inside the cave. "I have done as I was bidden, and now I leave you."

Before their eyes, the bones collapsed into a heap, sending up a small cloud of dust. The vast cavern spread out before them, and it seemed there were a million different routes to take. They did not know the location of their final destination.

"How could he have fulfilled his duty?" Taren asked in frustration. "We still don't know where the sorceress rests."

"I think we do," Zamna replied, pointing into the distance. All of the bridges converged at a single point ahead. An expansive plateau stretched itself beneath an unseen light source. Upon this plateau rested a circular dais with a rectangular-shaped stone at the center of it.

"Ailwen's tomb," Taren whispered, his eyes fixed on the sarcophagus. All that remained was to cross the bridges and make their way to the dais. It was only a matter of steps before he reached the symbol.

Chapter 18

Zamna stepped onto the bridge first, followed closely by Taren. The planks beneath their feet swayed slightly under their weight but held fast. Despite their advanced age, the planks appeared to be in excellent condition. Pools of sulfur bubbled beneath them, releasing clouds of foul-smelling gas into the air. The travelers paid it no heed. Zamna's mind focused on moving forward in hopes of finding treasure. His head turned in response to anything that glittered. Sadly, all he saw were traces of minerals shining under the magical light of the cavern.

Stepping up onto the plateau, they realized what they had seen from a distance had actually been a series of plateaus. There were several of them to be crossed before they reached the one that supported the sarcophagus. Each plateau along the way was graced by a series of statues, all depicting the same woman.

Stepping close to the first statue, Zamna asked, "Is this Ailwen?"

Taren did not know. "I have never seen a likeness of her," he admitted.

The glistening white-stone statue depicted a female in a flowing gown, her hands poised to cast a spell. Her face showed determination, her angular features displaying her beauty. Flowing freely on a permanent breeze, her chiseled strands of hair drifted more than a foot away from the statue.

To Zamna's disappointment, there were no jewels or other adornments on the statue. The figure did not interest him in the slightest. "Let's keep moving," he suggested.

Looking down from the next bridge revealed a deep chasm beneath them. Steam rose from the void below, but the pools of sulfur could not be seen.

"It's a long way down," Taren whispered, gripping tightly to the ropes at each side of the bridge.

Zamna, sure-footed as always, pressed on without looking down. The second plateau was home to two statues that faced opposite directions. Taren took a moment to observe them as well. They appeared to be the same woman, her hands outstretched as if casting magic throughout the vast cavern.

"She must have truly enjoyed looking at herself," Taren commented, smiling.

"Too bad she didn't enjoy gold or gems," Zamna muttered. So far he had found only a single sapphire, and that would not be enough to allow him to retire. The cavern appeared bare, with no signs of any fortune to be had. Frustrated, he marched on to the third plateau.

The statue that greeted the travelers showed a sorceress with her staff raised high, her flowing robe billowing on an unseen breeze. Frozen for eternity, she lifted her staff in defiance of her enemies, casting them down with her immense power. Taren stood in amazement, staring at the intense features displayed on the statue's face. Such concentration and strength, and absolute resolve, was almost intimidating. Though it was completely inanimate, he could feel the power radiating from the sculpted rock. Running his hand along its smooth surface, he was surprised to find that the stone was warm. The air inside the cavern was also warm, but for some reason he had expected the stone to feel cold. Its warmth only added to the awe he felt while gazing at it.

Zamna stepped forward, crossing his arms. "Excuse me," he said. "I hate to break this up, but we have a mission to complete."

Taren nodded, pulling his hand away from the statue. Crossing a final swinging bridge, they came at last to the fourth plateau, where the sarcophagus lay illuminated beneath an unseen light source. Zamna scanned the area for any sign of riches. No chests, no coffers, no piles of jewels or gems. There was nothing here for him. The tomb had already been stripped bare of its wealth, assuming there had ever been any to steal. Sighing with disappointment, he watched as Taren approached Ailwen's final resting place.

Carved upon the lid of the sarcophagus was the effigy of the same woman whose face adorned the many statues throughout the cavern. It appeared as though she were only resting, which surprised the young mage, considering the action poses of her other statues. This didn't seem to fit the vigorous lifestyle she obviously had led. Shining runes of silver displayed her name just below her feet. Taren rubbed a trembling hand across the chiseled letters. Ailwen lay before him.

"This is it!" he cried in excitement. "Finally!" He pushed with all his strength against the heavy stone lid, but it did not budge.

Zamna set aside his disappointment to lend some muscle to the task. Together they shoved, but the sarcophagus remained sealed.

"I'll have to use magic," Taren said. Reaching deep into his stores, he focused his energy to sliding the lid enough to peer inside the stone coffin. As he held the spell, a glint of gold inside caught his eye. Nearly losing his concentration, he focused once more, forcing the lid aside. It slid slowly to the side, landing heavily on the ground.

A cloud of dust rose out of the grave, and Taren fanned his hands to help clear it. His heart raced, and every vein in his body seemed to throb. This was his moment. The symbol was about to be his.

Taren could hardly breathe as he looked upon the remains of the once-great sorceress. Before him lay Ailwen in her skeletal form. Her bones were still arranged in the correct places, though her skin had long since rotted away. Nothing remained of her person but dried bones and dust. Upon her head she wore a simple, gold tiara. No magical staff, no jewels, and no other ornamentation graced her body. The symbol was not there. Taren's heart sank into his feet.

Clutched in the sorceress's bony hands was a scroll of parchment. Taren reached in to relieve the woman of her prize. Her grip held fast, and he had to pry her fingers away from the wooden ends of the scroll.

Noticing the look of utter despair on his friend's face, Zamna asked, "Is it what you were looking for?"

Taren shook his head. "Right tomb, wrong item." He raised the scroll to eye level, staring at it as if in a trance. He had come all this way for nothing. This scroll was probably the last laugh of the person who had taken the symbol away centuries ago. The thief had placed it there as a mockery to let the next person know he had already absconded with the prize.

Zamna saw the glint of gold from Ailwen's tiara. *Some gold is better than none*, he thought. With a single swipe, he snatched the golden crown from her head and tucked it inside his bag. Instantly, the ground began to quake, accompanied by a low rumbling sound. A deep crack appeared in the plateau only feet away from the sarcophagus.

Taren thrust the scroll into the pocket of his robe and ran toward the rope bridge. Zamna followed two steps behind, pausing as he reached the bridge. The crack continued to widen, and the rumbling became more of a groan. Before their eyes, a massive chasm formed where they once had stood. All went silent.

The travelers glanced at each other, their feet glued to the ground. Should they run? Would they ever find their way back to the entrance? Could there possibly be a back door they were supposed to use? With the bone man in a heap, there was no one left to guide them. Instead of running, they stood frozen, staring at the chasm.

A flash of shiny black scales leapt from the depths, its agile body moving silently across the plateau. They gaped in horror at the enormous figure. It was solid black and slender like a snake or an eel, its body stretching to a distance of at least thirty feet. At each end, a triangular head with two glowing yellow eyes stared back at them. Flicking its forked tongues, it tasted the air for its victims.

The duo raced across the bridge, not stopping to look back. When they reached the end of the bridge, Zamna grabbed his companion's arm, steering him along the plateau. Several feet ahead was a formation of massive columns that might protect them from the strange beast. The black creature pursued as the pair ran with all speed to the rock formations. Taking cover behind the solidified minerals, they paused a moment to catch their breath.

Taren tapped into his magic, preparing an energy blast for the approaching creature. It writhed and wriggled as it moved, and it was gaining ground on the pair, who were crouched behind the massive rocks. When the creature came into range, Taren unleashed the magic, sending the monster reeling. The pair took to their feet once more, their eyes scanning for a safer place to hide.

The beast regained its senses quicker than Taren had hoped. It was already searching for them as they fled. Taren paused a moment and summoned his magic. In his mind, he located the pile of bones left behind by their guide. Concentrating as best he could under stress, he animated the bones, rattling and clanging them to draw the creature away. The beast moved away to investigate, giving the pair enough time to make their escape.

They dashed along the plateau, moving farther and farther from the bridges that had brought them in. Deeper they ran inside the cavern, searching for anything that might shield them from their pursuer. Taren spotted a low shelf of minerals and pointed. Zamna followed him in, both men squeezing themselves inside the narrow opening between the lowered ceiling and the floor. With a blast of energy, Taren collapsed a stalactite to block the opening in front of them. There was no sign of the creature.

"What was that thing?" Zamna whispered.

"It's an amphista," Taren replied. "I've seen them only in bestiary books. I didn't think they really existed."

Zamna stared at him. "Apparently they do."

"They're said to be guardians of the Realm of the Dead," Taren explained. "Their bite is highly toxic. Usually its victims die without ever knowing they were bitten."

Zamna furrowed his brow. "We have to find a way out of this place."

The mage was not ready to leave. Though his hopes had been dashed, deep inside he knew the symbol must reside inside this tomb. He could not leave without it. If he had to search every inch to find it, that's what he would do. Master Imrit deserved that much from his apprentice. "The symbol could still be here somewhere," Taren replied. "I'm not ready to give up on it."

A hiss echoed from the walls of the cavern as the monster found its way to their location. The bones had not fooled it for long. Striking its massive head against the stone, it chipped away at the fallen rock that protected the men inside. Zamna drew his daggers, slashing at the massive head as it came forward. The amphista's tongue brushed his hand, leaving a sticky, foul-smelling residue.

"Keep your hands away from it!" Taren shouted. Reaching into his magic, he blasted energy toward the monster, knocking it slightly off-balance and moving the stone away. With the way ahead clear, the pair made their escape from the narrow space.

"What now?" Zamna asked as they ran into the darkened cavern.

"I have to find the symbol," the mage cried. "We need to go back to the burial site. I have to look for clues."

Zamna could understand the young man's frustration. He was frustrated as well. But with a giant snake chasing them, there was little chance of living long enough to find what they sought.

Turning down a corridor to their right, they stepped inside a tiny room. As the light caught up with their position, they beheld not one, but seven stone pillars, each standing at a different height. Laying low would not save them if they tried to cross the room.

"We can't go this way!" Zamna shouted. "Go back toward the grave. We'll see if there's another way out."

The amphista was approaching from behind them. It hissed, spitting a noxious substance at the pair. Instinctively, they dove in opposite directions to avoid the spray. Taren landed hard, smashing his shoulder against the wall. Rolling up to his feet, Zamna dashed to Taren and grabbed his arm. The mage was not as agile as the assassin, but fear proved a good motivator to ignore the pain he was in. They dashed forward, charging at the beast.

Taren extended a hand and focused his mind to paralyze the snake. This was their only chance to get past it. Summoning all the remaining power he had, he threw it at the monster. It reared its heads as the magic struck its lithe body. The force of the spell froze the beast in place, rendering it powerless as the two men ran by.

"How long will it stay like that?" Zamna asked, still running.

"Not long enough!" Taren replied. Cramming his hand into the pocket sewn inside his robe, he retrieved a potion. With a single gulp, he downed the liquid inside and tossed the vial over his shoulder. This was no time to be weakened by lack of power.

Racing through the massive cavern, they found their way back to Ailwen's grave. Without a care for respecting the dead, Taren dug greedily into her open sarcophagus, leaving her remains in disarray. Finding nothing, Taren fell to his knees defeated. Zamna stood tall, his daggers at the ready. The amphista could return at any minute.

"It's not here," Taren admitted quietly. "I've failed."

"What was on that scroll you found?" Zamna asked.

Taren had forgotten about the scroll. Retrieving it from his pocket, he opened it and stared at the words before him. It read as a letter from the sorceress to any who would disturb her tomb.

To the weary traveler,

It is all too likely you have come seeking the symbol which I possess, but I have not relinquished my claim to it. To the Realm of the Dead I have taken it. There it shall abide with me for eternity. Though it destroyed my body, I have melded the symbol with my own life essence, creating a synergy of unfathomable magic. No other sorcerer could hope to wield the power I have attained. Your journey has been for naught.

Ailwen, Mistress of Life and Death

Taren looked up from the scroll. "She's taken the symbol into the Realm of the Dead," he said dryly. "We'll never be able to retrieve it." Dropping his hands to the side, he allowed the scroll to fall to the ground.

While Taren read, Zamna scanned the walls behind the burial site for any sign of an exit. He chided himself for not having crafted a map of the path the bone man had led them on. Without knowing which route to take, they would likely never find their way out of the meandering tunnels. Peering down into the chasm where the amphista had appeared, Zamna asked, "Didn't you say that thing guarded the Realm of the Dead?"

Taren nodded, realizing what Zamna had in mind. "You think we should go down there?" he asked.

"There's no other way out," Zamna replied.

"The fall might kill us," Taren said.

"Then we'll be headed in the right direction." Zamna's face was serious, his eyes affixed on the depths of the chasm. There was no other choice. With the amphista on their trail, there was no time to get lost in the winding corridors. It would kill them long before they found the exit, assuming something else didn't get to them first.

A deafening screech ripped through the air. The amphista was moving again, and it was growing impatient. It flicked its red tongues to locate the prey it sought, and quickly homed in on their location. Charging forward, it slithered its way toward the intruders.

"We have to go now!" Zamna shouted. "It's the only way!"

Taren summoned his courage and nodded. Hoping the fall wouldn't kill them instantly, they ran for the chasm and jumped inside.

Chapter 19

Falling into the darkness, the two men could do nothing but lie back and experience the feeling of weightlessness. Down they fell, on and on. It seemed an eternity in the darkness as they continued to fall with no end in sight. The mists became thicker as they continued moving downward, but still no end came. As light as feathers, they floated along, their bodies lowering themselves within the mist. Finally, their bodies righted themselves, and the travelers landed softly with their feet against the floor.

They stared at each other a moment, neither understanding what had happened. Had they entered The Realm of the Dead? Had the fall killed them? Looking around in the darkness, they felt only minor relief that the monster had not followed them into the chasm.

Zamna stretched his arms out in front of him to make sure they were still there. "Are we alive?" he asked.

"I think so," Taren replied. He knew little of the Realm. To his knowledge, no one had returned from this place to write about it.

A thick fog settled around their feet, dissipating slightly as it rose higher into the air. All around them was darkness. Zamna focused his eyes to see, his night vision being superior to that of his companion.

"There are figures in the distance," he said. "I'm not sure what they are." Silently, he hoped the shapes ahead were not more amphistas.

Slowly they pressed on through the fog, Zamna leading the way. Only the smallest bits of light could be seen ahead of them as they faded in and out of view. Stumbling blindly, they proceeded toward the lights, hoping to find something — anything — that would lead them to the symbol.

Zamna's eyes scanned the darkness for any sign of an exit. This time he would not fail to mark its location. Becoming lost was not an option. The Realm of the Dead was no place for the living, though their descent had saved them from the amphista's deadly grasp.

Finally they reached the light, which shone down like a sliver of moon on a cloudy night. Though the poor lighting left much to be desired, they were grateful for the small amount of illumination. Footsteps paced slowly all around them, some of them shuffling and staggering. Puzzled, the two men paused, listening to the darkness.

Amid the footsteps, an occasional moan or cry could be heard. The sounds seemed far away at first but moved closer as the travelers maintained their position. A loud wail broke through the mixture of sounds. Somewhere, someone was weeping. The mournful sound sent a shiver down Taren's spine. The lights grew dimmer, leaving the men in utter darkness.

"We should keep moving," Taren whispered.

Without a word, Zamna moved forward, extending his hand in front of him to feel for unseen obstacles in his path. Only steps ahead, he bumped into a hard, cold object. Halting, he ran a hand across its surface. It appeared to be some type of rock, possibly obsidian by the feel of it. As he moved his fingers, he felt a lump sticking out of the rock at the level of his head. At that moment, the dim light returned, shining down onto the glassy rock. The face of a man, his features twisted in agony, appeared before them on the rock's surface. Zamna jumped back putting some distance between himself and the figure. His hand went instinctively to his dagger, but he did not draw it from its sheath. He could not use a blade to fight a man of stone.

Taren summoned his courage and stepped forward to observe the rock. There were no other body parts visible. Only the face of the tormented man could be seen. Taren wondered who this man had been and what he had done to deserve such a fate. Was this the death that awaited us all? With the light shining brighter, he stepped forward, ready to explore the rest of the Realm.

"Come on," the mage whispered.

Zamna took one last look at the face before proceeding. He could swear he saw its lips move, but maybe he was only imagining it. The lights grew dimmer once again, and Taren paused, placing a hand up to bar Zamna's path. The La'kertan looked up, seeing why the mage had stopped him.

A few yards ahead, spirits wandered aimlessly, their pale-purple forms moving silently on nonexistent feet. They seemed to hover rather than walk, but the sound of their footsteps could be heard against the cold stone floor.

"Maybe one of them can answer a few questions," Taren said. "I'm going to try talking to them."

Zamna was uneasy but made no move to stop the young man from trying. He had never fought a spirit before and had no idea if they could be harmful. As the light continued to move, it illuminated the path to the spirits. All along the walls, stony hands reached out with no visible sign of bodies. Their fingers extended outward as if grasping, locked in an eternal state of wanting. Zamna felt a chill. He knew what it was these hands wanted. They wanted his life essence to take as their own. It was life that they craved here in their world of darkness, and it was life that eluded them. Here were two lives that had come willingly to their abode.

"Don't let your guard down," Zamna cautioned. "And don't let those spirits touch you."

Taren nodded and approached one of the pacing spirits. It stepped back and forth, its head held between its hands.

"Excuse me," he said in a soft voice. "Can you help me?"

293

The spirit did not reply. It continued its pacing as if he were not there. Taren moved over to the figure of a woman. She sat silently against a black rock, her knees hugged tightly to her chest. Her head was bowed, and she appeared to be weeping. Taren knelt down beside her.

"Hello," he said. "Is there anything I can do for you?" He felt sorry for this spirit, who was obviously in need of comfort. The spirit did not look up. She continued to weep, unaware of his warm presence.

"I don't think they can see or hear us," Zamna said, coming to his friend's side.

Taren nodded in agreement. "Maybe we aren't really here."

Zamna seemed puzzled. "Not here?"

"Not to them, at least," he explained. "This is their Realm. We don't belong in it."

Zamna shook his head. He still did not understand, but it was of little consequence. He was anxious to get moving and find a way out.

The two men started to walk away, but Taren paused, turning his ear to the darkness. "Did you hear that?" he asked.

"Hear what?" the La'kertan asked, listening intently for the sound. All he heard was the pacing of the spirits and the weeping of the woman.

Taren hesitated a moment. "It sounded like music."

A distinct melody found its way to their ears. "I hear it!" Zamna said. "Do you recognize it?"

Taren nodded, still listening to the music. "It's the song of a nightingale," he said.

"Does it mean something?" Zamna asked. "Should we look for it?"

"In some tales, the nightingale represents immortality," the mage explained.

Zamna understood. If the bird meant immortality, then perhaps it could lead them to the symbol. After all, the sole purpose for retrieving it was to achieve immortality for Taren's master. "Let's find it then."

The song continued echoing through the darkness. The duo forged ahead, pointing themselves in the direction of the music. It grew louder as they approached, and eventually the figure of a small bird came into view. It flitted and flapped merrily upon the stones without a care in the world. Though it was only a spirit like the others in this Realm, it was neither mournful nor regretful. It seemed almost cheerful as it sang out to the darkness.

Taren approached the tiny creature with a half-smile. Stepping forward, he extended his hand to touch it. The bird evaporated, leaving behind a tiny puff of purple fog. A soft *clink* met Zamna's ears, and he approached the rock where the bird had been perched. His fingers groped in the darkness, feeling every inch of the stone surface. He stopped only when his hand landed on a small object, which he lifted toward the light. It appeared to be crystalline in structure, with a slight purple hue. The object was sharp, as if it had been sliced away from a larger stone. This piece was no more than a shard, about four inches long.

"It looks like it might be an amethyst," Taren said with a shrug.

"If it might be of value, then I'm taking it," Zamna replied, placing the shard in his pocket. Though small, it might fetch a good price should he ever escape from the Realm.

Taren did not care what became of the shard. It was the bird who had caught his interest, and now it was gone. The light dimmed once again, and Taren cursed the darkness. How would he ever find the symbol like this?

A single howl pierced the air, soon followed by more howls in response. Within seconds, an entire pack of wolves was howling somewhere in the darkness. Shadowy figures, outlined in pale purple, hurled themselves in the direction of the intruders.

"Run!" Zamna shouted.

Taren ran blindly, stumbling through the darkness. Desperately he tried to stay ahead of the pursuing wolves. Zamna constantly glanced over his shoulder to see if the mage was keeping pace. They ran with their hands out, groping desperately in the darkness to avoid colliding with unseen obstacles.

The wolves gained on them easily, their swift paws making easy strides along the dark passageway. They had no trouble seeing in total darkness; they were bred for this Realm alone.

Behind him, Zamna heard a crash as Taren tripped and toppled over onto the ground. The wolves were right behind him. Taren had no chance of escape. Drawing his daggers, Zamna ran back toward the mage, wondering how to fight an undead wolf.

The wolves reached Taren at the same time as Zamna. The assassin lashed out with the dagger in his right hand, immediately followed by the dagger in his left. The metal passed through the spirits without harming them. To his amazement, the wolves did not stop. Apparently, they had no interest in either of the men.

Helping Taren to his feet, he turned to watch as the wolves ran on ahead. Glancing at each other, the two proceeded to follow the pack. The light returned briefly, but long enough to give the travelers a glimpse at the spectacle ahead. The humanoid spirits were screaming in terror, fleeing from the pursuing wolves. They ran in all directions, some of them stumbling and falling. Without regard for the ones who had fallen, the others trampled them in their flight. The wolves bit into their legs, gnashing their teeth and tearing at the spirits. Though they were not creatures of mortal flesh, their agony was quite real. Zamna and Taren stared helplessly, unable to fathom the events taking place before them. The wolf hunt continued for several minutes before the beasts' appetites were satiated.

"We have to help them," Taren whispered. He stepped forward but stopped when he saw that the spirits who had been attacked were rising to their feet. Surprisingly, they went back to their normal routines of pacing aimlessly, and the wolves trotted along, leaving the spirits in peace.

Taren wondered who had sent the wolves, and if that person might be able to see and hear him. "We should follow the wolves," he suggested.

With no other course of action in mind, Zamna agreed.

The wolves headed back into the darkness, unhindered by the many obstacles in their path. They knew exactly where they were going, and they moved purposefully toward their destination. The two men pursued, their steps lit only by the soft purple glow of the spirit wolves.

Into the darkness they walked, seemingly for miles. Every step brought them closer to an unknown destination. Taren feared the wolves would simply disappear as the nightingale had, leaving him and his friend hopelessly lost. Twisting and turning, they continued on, leaving the other spirits farther behind.

"Maybe we should turn back," Zamna suggested. He had no idea how far they had gone, but it seemed they had been walking for hours. Perhaps the wolves had no destination in mind. Maybe they paced aimlessly as the human spirits did.

Taren wasn't sure what to do. They had come so far, it seemed pointless to turn back now. Where they had already been did not seem like the right place.

There had been no sign of the symbol nor an exit from the Realm. What harm could there be in pressing on? They were already lost. "Let's follow a while longer," he finally replied.

Zamna sighed. "Maybe they'll at least turn back when they're ready for another hunt."

Forward they trudged, still twisting and turning to avoid unseen obstacles in the blackness. They could no longer hear any sound but their own breathing. Even their feet ceased to make noise against the ground.

Zamna was about to insist they turn back when one of the wolves leapt, disappearing into a void of black. "What just happened?" he asked.

Taren did not reply. The two men watched as the wolves jumped one by one into the darkness, leaving the travelers alone to wonder.

"Great," Zamna said. "Just great!" Now they would have to travel back in the darkness without the aid of the nimble wolves.

Approaching the site where the wolves had disappeared, Taren reached out a hand. There was a wall, of sorts. It was not exactly solid. He could feel its resistance against his hand, but it had no texture whatsoever. Magic. This was a magical barrier, designed to keep certain individuals out while allowing others to enter.

"It's a portal," the mage said. "The wolves didn't disappear. They went through a gateway."

Approaching the barrier, Zamna asked, "What's on the other side?"

Taren did not know. Closing his eyes, he reached into his magic. Pulling just enough to sense where the portal might lead, he felt an intense burst of magical energy. Struggling to focus his mind, he tried to search deeper, but he could not. A series of intertwining lines filled his mind as they came together in a tight knot. It was the image of the symbol he had seen within the crystal cave. "The symbol!" he shouted. "We have to go through the portal." Without waiting for his companion to reply, he pushed his way through the barrier, disappearing within the darkness.

Chapter 20

Cautiously approaching the portal, Zamna stuck his arm inside first. Feeling no pain and only minimal resistance, he held his breath and pushed his way through. Taren stood on the other side, awaiting his companion's arrival. There was no sign of the wolves they had been following.

The entire space had a pale-orange glow, illuminating the dark with an eerie light. Ahead of them, the room branched out into corridors leading in every direction. There were no signs of anything living, no spirits, and no remains.

"Where are we now?" Zamna asked.

Taren could still see the symbol, its image burned in his mind. "I think I know what's going on here," he began. "I think Ailwen has taken over the Realm using the symbol. Those wolves were sent by her to torment the souls who dwell here."

"How do you know all that?" Zamna wondered. So far, Taren had known little more than he did. All of a sudden, he had an explanation. Had the mage been holding back on him the whole time?

"I don't know, exactly," the mage replied. "It's just a feeling I have. The symbol is here. I can feel its presence."

"Is it speaking to you? How do you know this isn't a trap?"

Taren wasn't sure. All he knew was that the same image he had seen in his vision had appeared to him here in the Realm. That couldn't be a coincidence. Unless, of course, someone had invaded his mind. Was Ailwen capable of such magic? It seemed likely she was. Taren shook the thought away, refusing to believe he had been manipulated. "The symbol is here. Even if it's a trap, I must keep moving forward."

With a sigh, Zamna nodded. So far he had come across little treasure and no exit. If he was going to escape this place, he would probably need the mage's skills at some point. He was determined to follow him and see it through, still hoping the journey might pay off.

As they stepped forward to observe the various paths they might take, Zamna felt a strange tingling in his side. The crystalline shard he had found was vibrating inside his pocket. Retrieving the purple shard, he held it in the palm of his hand. The shard began to spin like the needle on a compass. After several rotations, it halted, pointing down the northeast corridor.

"Do you think that might be the way to go?" the La'kertan asked.

Taren watched the shard intently. Taking it from his friend's hand, he held it between his thumb and forefinger. His first instinct was to cast a spell that would help him determine the composition of the crystal. As he reached for his magic, the shard sent out a spark. Nearly dropping it from the shock, he did his best to hold onto it. An image of the symbol filled his mind. He could see it clearly, turning over itself as it hurled its way through the darkness, disappearing only when it reached his face.

Taren nodded quickly. "Yes, I do think we should go where the shard was pointing," he said, handing it back to the assassin. "Make sure you keep that close. It's more than just a gem." He wasn't sure what the crystal was, but it obviously held some significance.

They stepped into the passageway, which was lit with the same pale-orange light. The walls appeared sickly, thanks to the strange light, and it gave the travelers an uneasy feeling. The air itself felt diseased, the sickness wafting throughout the passageway. They pressed on, their footsteps echoing through the corridor.

Halting as they reached the end of the hallway, they could clearly see a brighter light in front of them, illuminating a room ahead. A booming voice sounded from inside, "I've been waiting for you." A deep, throaty laugh followed the words.

The two men exchanged glances. Clearly someone inside was aware of their presence. Zamna placed a hand over his pocket, attempting to still the vibrations of the crystal, which had begun buzzing at the sound of the voice.

"What do we do?" he asked.

"We go inside," Taren replied. The symbol was waiting for him. He could almost feel its warmth in his hands.

Moving forward, the pair entered a vast, circular room littered with massive black boulders and rock formations of various shapes. A solitary figure stood at the center of the room on a raised, black-stone dais.

Before their eyes, the figure began to grow, reaching a height of at least ten feet. Locks of raven hair cascaded down the figure's back. Turning to reveal her face to her guests, the sorceress flashed a smile. Her pale, milky skin contrasted against her dark hair, and she wore a flowing gown of black and red. The dress was tattered and worn at the end, but there were no feet to be seen. Instead, she floated several inches above the ground, her arms spread wide in welcoming.

"Poor little wizard," her voice boomed. "He's come so far in search of the symbol." A wicked laugh escaped her throat.

Taren boldly stepped forward. "I have indeed," he stated. This was Ailwen who stood before him. He was sure of it. Her face was the same as he had seen on the numerous statues throughout her tomb and upon her sarcophagus. Her beauty was undeniable, as was her power. It practically radiated from her, and he could feel it tingling against his skin.

"So brave," Ailwen replied. "But you could not wield the symbol, even if I were to give it to you. You are far too weak." Another laugh echoed throughout the room.

Zamna pressed the shard to his side in an attempt to stop its incessant vibrations. Why had the sorceress not attacked? Did she consider them so insignificant? The La'kertan crouched low, one hand poised over his dagger. Her mood might change at any moment, and he was prepared.

Taren stood tall, facing the sorceress. He had no desire to sound boastful. If she wanted to believe him too weak to retrieve the symbol, so be it. He was a master wizard now, and he no longer doubted his own abilities. If it came down to it, he was determined to fight to the death to retrieve the symbol. Dying here was far better than returning home empty-handed.

As if reading his mind, Ailwen said, "You're prepared to fight, and I commend you. You will undoubtedly fail. I possess the symbol, and you wouldn't be a match for me even without it." She blasted a charge of silver magic through the air, aiming it at Taren's feet. He jumped back in time to avoid being hit, but quickly regained his footing and stood tall.

"The symbol has come to me in a vision," Taren stated. "It calls to me." Perhaps her resolve would weaken if she thought he was destined to take the symbol from her.

Ailwen only laughed louder at his words. Halting her laughter, she bent low, bringing her face close to his. "It was the symbol that bound me to this place. I wasn't prepared for the immensity of its power." She backed away from the mage, returning to her original location at the center of the room. "My servant placed the scroll with my remains to lure you here. Now that I have you, I can use your life essence to return to my natural state. I shall live again!"

A thunderous clap of magic rattled the room, and Taren instinctively rolled to one side. A large chunk of ceiling crashed down on the exact spot where he had been standing. Zamna moved to his side, helping him back to his feet. The two stayed low as they crept into a dark corner, concealing themselves behind a massive boulder.

"It will go easier with your cooperation," Ailwen said with a laugh. "But I shall have you nonetheless. My servant was disappointed when you escaped his grasp." With a swirl of black magic, she conjured the amphista. It reared its heads, both tongues flicking out to locate the intruders who had previously escaped it.

Looking over his shoulder at the massive beast, Zamna said, "I'll try to get its attention. You stay here and blast the damn thing!"

"Wait—" Taren started to say. Too late. Zamna had already bolted from his position of safety and was running toward the amphista.

Zamna paused halfway to the creature and stamped his feet against the stone. Clapping his hands together loudly, he screamed, "Come and get me!"

The scaly black heads turned to face their prey, and instantly the beast set off to give chase. Zamna ran hard, forming a wide circle around the room. He was fast, but the amphista was faster. The La'kertan would have to outmaneuver it as he darted and dodged among the rocks.

Taren summoned his magic and focused on his target. It was moving ahead at a determined pace, but he was sure he could hit it. Muttering the incantation for a lightning spell under his breath, he thrust his hands forward to release the blast. It missed only inches away from the creature.

Ailwen shrieked with laughter at Taren's failure. "You'll have to do better than that," she said mockingly. "Run little lizard, or he'll catch you!" Her laughter continued as she watched the spectacle in front of her.

If not for his pursuer, Zamna would have fallen over, grasping his head in frustration. How could

Taren miss? This was no time for practice. He had personally witnessed what the mage could do. With all his energy focused on staying alive, he could only continue to run to evade the amphista. It struck at his side, and the La'kertan instantly dropped and rolled to his left, narrowly missing the venomous fangs. Coming smoothly back to his feet, he shifted course, squeezing himself between two skinny rock formations. They glistened with runes in the orange light, but Zamna had no time to stop to observe them. The amphista continued its pursuit, maneuvering expertly around the rocks.

Taren reached for his magic again, forcing himself not to dwell on his mistake. With a deep breath, he cleared his mind and summoned the lightning. This bolt struck the center of the amphista, flipping it on its side and giving Zamna the chance to sprint ahead.

Zamna felt a moment of relief as he put some distance between himself and his attacker. He hadn't expected a beast so massive to be so agile. Taren was already casting another spell, bombarding the giant black serpent with wave after wave of energy. It could no longer keep its course, so it turned and headed directly for Taren. Zamna swung around and pursued

311

the monster, hoping that Taren could at least hold it still long enough for him to stab it a few times.

Instead, Taren reached down and focused his mind to his magic. Remembering how he had succeeded in entering the tomb, he began the lightning spell with his left hand. Releasing the magic, it dug itself into the flesh of the oncoming creature. With his right hand, he summoned fire. The blast was weaker than the lightning, but he felt certain it would be enough. Allowing the red magic to fly from his fingers, it seared at the creature's flesh. The amphista halted its advances, both massive heads writhing in pain. Taren held the spell as long as he could, but finally his concentration was broken. He opened his eyes to see if the beast still lived. As he watched, it shriveled, coiling itself into a pile on the floor.

Zamna reached it just in time to witness its demise. With a nod of approval, he slowly made his way back to Taren's side.

Ailwen's voice boomed, "No! My child!" With a roar of anger, she began to conjure, black magic swirling all around her.

Zamna stared at the sorceress, his eyes wide. "You've got to stop her!" he shouted.

Taren knew he couldn't let her cast her spell. Though his magic reserves were low, he had to act. Summoning every ounce of power remaining to him, he began the first spell. His right hand dug deep into his roots as an earth mage, sending out a thick beam of green light. With his left hand, he summoned a blast of white hot air. Focusing his mind to the sorceress, he desired nothing more than to stop her from finishing the spell she had begun. An image of the symbol burst into his mind, filling all of his thoughts. Still he held fast, the magic flying from his fingertips. When he could hold it no longer, the magic stopped, and he buckled to his knees.

Zamna saw his chance to act. The sorceress had taken a massive hit, and she had returned to her normal size. Instead of standing ten feet tall, she was no bigger than the average woman. Her body rocked, swaying unbalanced upon the platform.

Running at top speed, Zamna retrieved the crystalline shard from his pocket. It pulsated with energy and glowed with a pale-purple light. It knew its purpose, as did Zamna. In an instant, he leapt to the stone dais where the sorceress stood, burying the shard deep into the back of her neck.

With a shrill, piercing shriek, Ailwen exploded in an intense burst of light. Both Zamna and Taren flew backward, struck by a massive wave of energy. Zamna landed unscathed along the floor, but Taren was thrown against the wall, hitting his head in the process. He lay unconscious upon the stone floor.

Zamna rose to his feet and approached the dais. The sorceress left behind neither blood nor a body. Only a faint pile of yellow dust remained where she once stood. Zamna reached down to sweep the pile away. Instead of softness, his fingers encountered a hard, metal object. He lifted it from the pile and wiped the dust from it. A series of metal strands wove themselves in and out to form a tight knot on this seemingly insignificant piece of jewelry. With a smile, the La'kertan realized what he was holding.

Descending from the platform, he made his way over to his companion. Taren was sitting up, a vial of potion held feebly in his hand. He downed it in two sips and looked up in time to see his friend approaching.

Zamna stuck a claw in between two of the metal strands, allowing the symbol to hang freely from his finger. Dangling it before the young mage, he asked,

"Is this what you're looking for?" A grin spread over his lips.

Taren's eyes went wide as he beheld the symbol he had seen in his vision. It glistened in the pale-orange light. Reaching up, he took the symbol in his hand. It was warm to the touch and had a natural feeling to it that he could not explain. It felt like it belonged in his hand and had always been a part of him. He had succeeded and could now return to his master.

"I kept my eyes open for an exit while I was running from that snake," Zamna said, snapping Taren back to reality. "I didn't see one."

Taren stared at the trinket in his hand. "Maybe the symbol can help us find a way."

"Do you know how to use it?" Zamna asked.

Taren shook his head. "I can't say that I *know*, but I feel like it wants to help me. I can hear its voice in my head, but I don't understand it."

Zamna had never studied magic, but at times, his matter-of-fact attitude could prove wise. "Maybe you don't need to know how to use it then. If it's willing to help you, just tell it what you want."

"I want nothing more than to return to my master," Taren said. "But you still haven't found what you were looking for."

Zamna shrugged. "There's no helping that," he declared. "There were no riches here to find."

Taren stood and squeezed the symbol tightly in his hand. Focusing his mind, he found his thoughts to be full of images of the interwoven metal strands. Every attempt to calm his mind failed. He could not release his mind from the symbol. It occurred to him that perhaps that was how the symbol worked. It would fill his mind and carry out his desires. Focusing his mind to the symbol, he thought, *My friend and I wish to leave this place.*

In a blinding flash of light, the two men were teleported away from the Realm of the Dead to a room inside Ailwen's tomb. It was not one they had seen before. Taren observed the walls and realized there was a door, and light was visible at its edges.

Zamna noticed something else. The ground was littered with small bits of metal. Stooping to retrieve one, he brushed the dust away before biting down on it. "Gold," he said. "There are gold pieces on the floor." Frantically, he began to collect them. Taren smiled but did not budge. "You can have a few," the La'kertan said. "There are so many." He couldn't believe his luck.

"You take them," Taren insisted. He already had what he came for. Rubbing his fingers over the symbol, he realized how beautifully crafted it was. The surface was smooth and soft, but it held a magical heat to it that felt soothing in his hand.

Zamna placed the gold pieces inside his pack and searched the ground a second time to ensure he had found them all. Mages surely had need of money, but if Taren did not want to take any for himself, then that was his choice. The La'kertan was content to take his share of the tomb's treasure. Though it wouldn't be enough to live a life of luxury, it was a considerable sum.

Taren lifted the symbol toward the door, not bothering to read the runes carved upon it. With this device, he would not need to figure out another puzzle. The door slid aside, obeying the command of the powerful object, and sunlight filled the room.

The two men stepped out into the strange land of red-brown soil. A hazy red fog filled the sky, but the sun's rays filtered their way through it, brightening the otherwise dreary land. Behind them, the stone door sealed itself, leaving no trace of where it had been. The pair found themselves near one of the many corridors of the compound.

"I would never have guessed there was a door here," Zamna said.

"It was probably accessible only from inside," Taren replied. Looking at his friend, he asked, "Will you come with me to Ky'sall?" After so much time spent together, he was in no hurry to part from his friend. There were still many things he did not know about him, and he hoped they would remain friends for many long years.

Zamna shook his head. "I have some things to attend to, and then I think I'll go home," he said. "I'd like to see my family again."

Taren could respect that. "The symbol will likely take me anywhere I tell it. Would you like to go to La'kerta now?"

Again, Zamna shook his head. "I have unfinished business in Rixville. I can make my own way home after I've done what needs doing."

Taren hoped the business did not involve murder, but he decided it was best not to ask. Without questioning his friend further, he focused his energy to the symbol. With a flash of light, the men arrived only feet from the wooden walls of Rixville.

Chapter 21

A few citizens took notice of the travelers' strange arrival. It wasn't every day they witnessed people appearing from thin air. They peered at the odd pair curiously for a moment before returning to their own affairs. The guards eyed them suspiciously but apparently recognized the La'kertan.

One of them nodded in his direction. "Ye've got some interestin' friends," he said.

Zamna shrugged and looked away. The guards returned to their difficult work of leaning against the city walls.

Though Taren's stomach was begging for a hot meal, he was anxious to return home to his master. Turning to face Zamna, he said, "I'm going to miss having you around." He meant those words. After weeks of traveling side by side, taking turns rescuing each other, and sharing strange meals and stories, Taren would have to readjust to life without his friend.

Zamna replied with a smirk and a shake of his scaly head. Long goodbyes were not his style. Though he considered Taren a friend, it was now time to part company. The life of an assassin was constantly changing, and this was just another step along his road. "Take care of yourself," he said, slapping the young mage on his back.

"You too," Taren replied. He watched as the La'kertan walked away, eventually blending into the crowd of Rixville's citizens. He hoped he would see Zamna again someday, but his own future was uncertain. There would be much to do once he returned home. He might be studying the symbol with Imrit for many years to come. That would leave little time for travel or visiting with friends. If he was lucky, Imrit would have all the answers waiting for him when he returned home. Knowing the old man, he had probably worked nonstop since sending the apprentices away. Taren's only regret was that he would have to deliver the bad news about Tissa and Djo.

Taren turned his back to the town and clutched the symbol tightly in his hand. Focusing his mind, he thought, *I'm ready to go home.* Nothing happened. Wrinkling his brow, Taren shrugged away the failure and tried again. Picturing Imrit's cottage in is mind, he concentrated on the symbol. It warmed in his hand but didn't take him from his current location.

Holding the metal object close to his face, he turned it over to allow the light to fall on its various strands. Another picture came into his mind. He could clearly see The Barrens. A shudder ran through his body as he remembered the stone beast and the death of his companions. Imrit had warned against the use of magic in the ancient forest. Could that be why the symbol was not working? The Barrens was an ancient land, and an unknown enchantment had been placed over it. Were the two ancient magics at odds with each other? If Imrit's studies were correct, the symbol would be slightly younger than The Barrens. Either it had its limitations, or Taren was not able to use it properly. Whichever scenario was correct mattered not at this point. The mage would have to cross through the forest on foot.

Shifting his pack to a more comfortable position, he began to walk. The ground here was still covered with vibrantly colored patches of mossy grass, and it felt soft and familiar underfoot. If there were time, Taren would have liked to study the region to determine what sort of magic was responsible for its strange appearance. But that would have to wait. He must return the symbol to his master.

It wasn't long before his feet brought him to the edge of The Barrens. The towering trees formed an almost impenetrable line, the yellow-brown soil starkly contrasting against the vivid colors of the land beneath his feet. Taking a deep breath, he peered between the trees, wondering if the stone beast was still waiting for him. He tucked the symbol into his pocket, for fear its magic might attract the creature. Without knowing how to use its power, he wasn't sure if it would help or hurt the situation should the beast appear. He swallowed hard, his heart rate rising. He had outrun it once before, and he could do it again. Unfortunately, if the beast appeared early, the distance back to the cottage was much farther than he had to run the previous time.

With little choice, he stepped between the trees, immersing himself in the poorly lit forest. He spotted the path immediately and remembered to stay off it. Staying slightly left of the path, he began the slow march back home. There were several obstacles in the form of fallen branches, and his pace was moderate. He desperately wished to clear the forest quickly, but walking faster resulted only in his stumbling and nearly falling to the ground.

With sadness, Taren wondered if he would come across the remains of his former companions. If so, they deserved a proper burial, and he would take the time to give them one. Tissa had fallen close to the exit, but there was no sign of her body. Taren paused and carefully observed his surroundings, but nothing of the apprentice remained. The young mage did not care to think what might have become of her at the hands of the beast.

He trudged on, finding no sign of Djo either. The two apprentices had shared the same fate, and there was no trace of either of them. Was it at all possible they had survived and returned to the cottage? Though unlikely, the thought gave Taren a momentary feeling of hope. In the back of his mind, however, he knew that was not the case. He had seen the stone beast slashing at his companions, and he knew they would not survive. Had he been wrong to flee and leave them to their fate? What could he have done to save them? The regret would always be with him.

As the light began to fade, a soft pink glow broke through the treetops. Taren felt a sudden surge of fear, knowing he would have to spend the night alone in The Barrens. To his surprise, the symbol warmed in his robe pocket. Taren's heart began to pound. Wrenching the item from his pocket, it glistened in the dim light. It was using magic.

Taren stood frozen, not knowing from which direction the beast would come. He could not run until it showed itself, or he risked running straight into its waiting claws. Soon, the stone beast appeared before him, its black eyes locking onto his. Instinctively, Taren lifted the symbol over his head, his feet rooted firmly to the ground. This time, he would not run. He would fight.

The beast had something else in mind, however. After staring at Taren for a moment, it turned its back and calmly walked away, disappearing among the trees. Taren lowered the symbol and observed it. It flashed with a multitude of lights before fading back to its original gold color. Whatever the symbol had done, it had saved him from the beast. After returning it to his pocket, he continued his march.

Taren walked through the night, not bothering to stop and rest. All his thoughts focused on returning home, and he could not have slept, even if he had wanted to. The symbol continued to put off heat as it rested in his pocket, refusing to cease the magic it had started when he encountered the beast.

As morning broke through the trees, Taren realized where he was. The area before him looked familiar. This was the spot where he had paused to look back at his master's cottage. The trees formed a straight line just ahead of him. Somehow the symbol had shortened the journey by days. He was home.

Pushing past the trees, Taren's eyes beheld the stone cottage that had been his home. A soft plume of white smoke rose lazily from the chimney, disappearing into the blue sky above. Near the well, Vita was drawing water. The mage smiled, his heart full of gladness to be back where he belonged.

Lifting the heavy water bucket, Vita heard someone approaching. Swiveling around, she recognized Taren immediately. Dropping the bucket, she ran to him and hugged him tightly. "It's good to have you home," she said, still squeezing him.

"It's good to be here," he replied.

Vita backed away and asked, "Where are Tissa and Djo?"

Taren looked at the ground. "They didn't make it," he said, his tone somber.

Vita brought her hands up to cover her mouth, her eyes filling with tears. Choking back a sob, she said, "I'm sorry to hear that." With a deep breath, she said, "Come inside. Master Imrit will be delighted to see you."

The two walked slowly into the cottage. Imrit was not sitting at his desk near the window as Taren expected.

"Is he in the laboratory?" he asked.

Vita shook her head. "He hasn't been well," she informed him. "He's taken to his bed."

Taren felt like he'd been struck with a hammer. "It's that bad?" he asked. Imrit had never been one to sit for long, let alone lay abed. A lump rose to Taren's throat as he realized his master was gravely ill.

Vita patted the young mage on his shoulder. "His age is catching up with him, I think," she said with a weak smile. "Your presence will bring him cheer."

The pair entered Imrit's bedchamber. Vita knocked at the doorframe to alert him of their presence.

"Look who's come home," she said, approaching the bed. Assisting the elderly wizard to sit up, she added, "Taren is here." Grabbing at the pillows that had been strewn about, she propped him up, allowing him to sit comfortably without effort.

Taren slowly approached the old man and knelt next to the bed. "I've got the symbol, Master."

Imrit reached out his bony hands, placing them on either side of Taren's face. He stared into the young man's eyes and smiled. "You're home," he said. Weakly he leaned forward to embrace his student.

Taren hugged him back, being careful not to squeeze too tightly. Then, he reached into his pocket to retrieve the symbol. It radiated heat on his hand. Offering it to his master, he watched as the old man's eyes gleamed.

His fingers caressing the metal, Imrit said, "Master Taren, you've done something extraordinary."

Taren beamed with pride. "I did it for you, Master. You can use this to make yourself well. You can live forever." Taren desired nothing else. Imrit meant more to him than anyone in the world, and he could not bear to think of his death.

Imrit closed his eyes and shook his head slowly. "I no longer have the strength to use this," he said, handing the symbol back to his former apprentice. "You are a master wizard now. You must unlock its potential on your own."

"But, Master—" Taren started to say.

Imrit held up a hand to silence him. "I have made my peace with this world," he began. "The symbol is in capable hands. I'm ready to move on."

Tears welled in Taren's eyes. He could no longer contain his grief. Everything he had gone through was for Imrit. He did not desire the symbol for himself. How could he possibly hope to understand its power without Imrit to guide him? "Master," he said, "I know so little of the symbol. I can't possibly study it without you."

Imrit laughed softly. "You can, and you must," he replied. Leaning back against his pillow, he said, "Ailwen tried to rule over the symbol and force it to her will. That's why it abandoned her." He glanced at the mage with a slight grin on his face.

Taren did not understand. How had the symbol abandoned Ailwen? Is that why it did not protect her from Zamna's attack? His master's words only created confusion in his mind.

Imrit continued to explain. "What needs to be done is for a mage to become one with the symbol. The two must exist as equal parts of a whole." He leaned up on his arm to look at Taren. "When it knew you were coming for it, it began imprinting itself on you. It grew tired of Ailwen's dominance, and it craved a new master: you. All that remains is for you to claim it as your own."

Now it made sense. All the images of the symbol that had clouded his mind and every time he had sensed its presence. All of it was real. The symbol wanted him to take it—to use it as his own. He looked down at the symbol in his hands, its golden surface shining brightly. The image of his own reflection came through clearly. *How can I claim it as my own when it rightly belongs to him?*

Imrit began to cough, and Vita rushed to his side. Pressing a glass of water to his lips, she held his head as he took a sip. "He should rest now," she said quietly.

Taren nodded. Rising to his feet, he placed the symbol on the nightstand next to his master's bed. There it would remain until Taren was prepared to claim it. That day was not today. There were potions he could craft that would bring his master comfort, and that was far more important to him.

Over the next several days, Taren spent every waking moment at his master's side. Along with Vita, he tended to the ailing man's every need. Imrit died peacefully, clutching the hand of the young man he had raised as a son. Taren grieved for him, but there was nothing he could do. No spell in his power could bring back this man whom he had loved as a father. Imrit had accepted the ending of his life, and Taren would have to as well. In time, the pain would lessen, but he would carry his master in his heart always.

A few days after Imrit breathed his last, Taren returned to the old man's room to retrieve the symbol. It sat where he had left it, patiently awaiting his return. There had been no strange images invading his mind. Instead, the symbol had allowed him peace while he mourned. Now it gleamed with a golden light, anxious to become one with the wizard.

Taren lifted the symbol in his hand. Now that Imrit was gone, there was no other who had a claim to it. Taking a deep breath, he said, "I am Master Taren, and I bind you to me. We shall be as one, our powers uniting for all time."

The symbol flashed red, its searing heat burning into Taren's hand. He panicked momentarily, wondering if he had misspoken. As the heat became more intense, Taren attempted to drop it, but it held fast to his skin. Raising his right arm, he watched as the symbol burned itself into his flesh, disappearing beneath his skin. Blackened lines surrounded his hand, weaving their way up his arm. He and the symbol were now one.

About the Author

Lana Axe lives in the Missouri countryside surrounded by dogs, cats, birds, and reptiles. She spends most of her free time daydreaming about elves, magic, and faraway lands.

For more information, please visit: lana-axe.com.